"You spied on me!"

Valerie felt her face grow warm as she spoke. To think Roger had watched her take off all her clothes and frolic in the stream!

Roger laughed incredulously. "Spy on you? Damn it, Valerie. You were gone a long time and I was worried about you."

"So that gave you the perfect excuse to be a voyeur?"

"I never intended to spy on you. Please, will you forgive me?"

Valerie eyed him with resentment. Then she shrugged and said primly, "Very well. We do have to work together after all."

"That didn't sound too sincere to me," he put in reproachfully as he started toward her. "Let's make up."

Valerie felt highly unsettled yet suddenly aroused as he stalked her. Backing away, she stammered, "Just because you saw me doesn't mean you can . . ."

Roger quickly closed the distance between them and crushed her against his solid stren_____ On the contrary, Valerie, it do__

Eugenia Riley is the author of ten historical and contemporary romances, but *Love Nest*, her first Temptation, is a very special novel. Her husband Sterling is an avid bird-watcher, and he helped with the research. And during the writing, she and Sterling celebrated their twentieth wedding anniversary. To add to this labor of love, Eugenia chose historic Natchez, Mississippi, as the setting, which to her is the most romantic place in the world.

Eugenia Riley lives in her native Texas with her husband and their two teenage daughters.

Love Nest

EUGENIA RILEY

Harlequin Books

TORONTO • NEW YORK • LONDON
AMSTERDAM • PARIS • SYDNEY • HAMBURG
STOCKHOLM • ATHENS • TOKYO • MILAN

To Sterling—
who taught me to love birds,
and so much more.

Published March 1990

ISBN 0-373-25392-3

1

VALERIE VERNON UTTERED a groan of frustration as she sloshed through the front door of Vernon's Camera Shop, her dripping camera bag hanging from her shoulder, her tripod beneath her arm.

"Practically had to rent a rowboat to make it to the Tot Lot!" she declared to her father as she whipped around behind the counter, gently placing her equipment on the long, padded bench against the wall. Unsnapping her rain hood, she continued dramatically, "Then when I get there, the little darlings are climbing the walls from having had no play period this morning. As soon as I get three of them seated, four of them pop up like Mexican jumping beans!" Straightening, Valerie hung her slick yellow raincoat on the coat tree behind her, rolling her eyes at her father as she asked, "Why do I take on these assignments for school pictures, anyway?"

Standing near her behind the glass display case, Valerie's balding father chuckled softly and laid his pipe down in an ashtray. "Now, Val, show a bit of tolerance—you were a tot once yourself, or have you forgotten? And don't you want a husband and kids of your own someday?"

"Yes to both," Valerie admitted with a half smile, adding skeptically, "if the right man comes along." Stretching on tiptoe, she planted a kiss on her father's cheek, smelling the familiar aromatic essence of his custom-mixed pipe tobacco. Ruefully she added, "Though surely I'll not be blessed with a dozen mischievous moppets like those I contended with today."

Valerie's broad-faced father smiled wistfully as he pointed out, "Your ma always did say you were into more mischief than triplets. I'll never forget the time when you were four and set the lawn sprinkler inside our brand new car—then proceeded to turn it on."

Valerie smiled as she shook moisture from her long mane of auburn hair. Tilting her oval face toward her father in a quizzical attitude, she inquired softly, "You miss those days, don't you, Dad?"

Fred Vernon nodded solemnly. To Valerie, he suddenly looked very old and tired, his gray eyes obscured by the glare of light on his steel-rimmed glasses. "I miss your ma."

Valerie felt a tightening in her chest at her father's words. Mary Vernon had been dead for only a year, and grief still gnawed at them both. Valerie cleared her throat and bravely changed the subject. "Any calls for me?"

Her father shook his head. "Sorry, Val."

Biting her lip, Valerie laid a tightly clenched fist atop the display case, with great restraint resisting the urge to slam her hand against the glass. "Blast!" she muttered, pent-up frustration in her tone. "The man from *Southern Times* promised he'd call me three days ago about that assignment—either way, he said. You'd think by now—"

"By now he's hired someone else, Val," her father pointed out gently, laying a broad hand over his daughter's clenched fist.

Valerie nodded desolately, her blue eyes darkening with disappointment. "But he should have had the decency to call."

"He should have. But that's the way of the world, honey. You can't change it."

"It just makes me so angry. My portfolio's as impressive as that of any photographer in the state—and I'm a native of Natchez, to boot. I've photographed every antebellum home in the city, and I know the Delta country like the back of my hand."

"Val, Val," her father soothed, shaking his head. "We've been over this a thousand times, sweetheart. Your work is excellent, but you just don't have the credits as yet. And you're not advancing your cause by staying here in Natchez year after year—"

"Dad, we've been over that, too," Valerie interrupted firmly. "I can't leave Natchez." Before her father could protest, she added, "I mean, I don't *want* to leave."

Fred Vernon eyed his daughter sternly. "Are you still holding out hope that young scoundrel from Laurel will come crawling back to you with his tail between his legs?"

Valerie felt herself paling, but shook her head and quickly replied, "Heavens no, Dad. It's been over between Mark and me for two years now."

"I'd still like to get my hands on that rapscallion," Fred went on grimly. "He did something to you, Val. You haven't been quite the same ever since."

Valerie swallowed hard, knowing that in a sense her father had spoken the truth. At last she said, "It wasn't just Mark. There was Mom...."

Fred nodded. "I know, dear, I know." He forced a smile and added, "So now you're sticking around to take care of your old man, eh?"

"Why not?" she asked with a flash of spirit, giving her dad a warm hug.

"You're far too good to this old bag of bones," Fred grumbled, hugging her back. Yet he was grinning with pride as he returned to his stool and picked up the camera he'd been working on earlier. "And don't worry about that fella from the magazine. You've got what it takes and you're going to make it to the top. One day, opportunity will walk through your door, and you'll laugh at all of this."

"I hope so," Valerie said with a determined grin. Eyeing her limp hair and damp clothing with distaste, she added, "Though if opportunity does walk through my door, I hope it won't be today. I look like a flood refugee."

Then, as if on cue, the door to the camera shop flew open, and the rain ushered in a tall dark stranger carrying a battered aluminum case.

Valerie and her father exchanged meaningful glances as the dripping, scowling man strode across the tile floor toward the counter, laying the mangled case next to Fred Vernon's work area.

Barely suppressing a giggle as she recalled her father's last remark, Valerie swept around the counter to greet their customer. As she approached, the man pivoted slightly to stare at her, still frowning. With a slight flutter in her stomach, she realized that he was very handsome. His tan good looks bespoke the outdoorman, but his clothing was strictly Madison Avenue. He wore a smartly tailored all-weather coat and carried a stylish black umbrella with an ebony handle. Noting that his dark brown hair was streaked with gray about the sideburns and temples, Valerie judged him to be at least forty, quite a bit older than she. He was above average height, and though Valerie was taller than most women, she found herself having to look up at him slightly. He wore dark-rimmed glasses, which, coupled with his square jaw and cleanly cut features, gave him a rather intimidating bearing.

She started to speak, but found herself arrested by his deepset brown eyes as he appraised her steadily from behind the glasses. Then his gaze darkened perceptibly and he smiled just slightly. An unbidden shiver of excitement swept through her. She knew that this man liked what he saw.

Actually Valerie was accustomed to the perusal of the opposite sex; men were often attracted by her auburn hair and long legs. And Mark used to say her figure was "just curvy enough to be voluptuous." Since the unhappy breakup with Mark, she had become largely immune to the unsolicited scrutiny of strangers; yet somehow she found this man's gaze particularly unsettling, even titillating. There was something very commanding about him.

She moved closer and was horrified to hear a squishing sound emanating from her feet. Glancing downward, she noted with dismay that she had forgotten to remove her rain-soaked galoshes. Looking back up at him, she lamely offered, "May I take your coat and umbrella, sir? I'm sure you're half-soaked."

For a moment the stranger's attention was drawn to Valerie's bright yellow rain boots, and a trace of amusement pulled at his stern mouth. Then he glanced up at her. "Yes, miss," he said in a deep, businesslike voice. "Thank you." He removed his coat and handed it to her with his umbrella.

Minus his raincoat, the newcomer looked casually elegant in navy flannel slacks and a tan pullover sweater. Self-consciously Valerie moved away to hang his coat, hearing her father greeting the man. "Well, sir, a customer is a blessed sight during this downpour."

While the two men exchanged comments on the April weather in Natchez, Valerie placed their customer's coat and umbrella on the rack behind the counter, then quickly bent over to remove the offending galoshes.

"Hmmm," she heard that same deep voice murmur a moment later, "I approve."

Belatedly Valerie realized the sight she must pose, bent over with her derriere displayed by damp jeans that hugged her bottom like wet canvas drying on a frame. She hastily straightened, auburn curls falling about her hot face as she glanced suspiciously at the newcomer. Yet his frowning brown eyes were firmly fixed on the shelves above her as he scrutinized cameras, telephoto lenses and strobes.

"Yes," the stranger was now gravely continuing to Valerie's father, "I'm pleased to see that at least one merchant in Natchez runs an adequately stocked camera shop."

With a puzzled frown, Valerie leaned over to quickly strip off her galoshes. She caught a glimpse of her father laying down his work. "I'm Fred Vernon. The young lady who just greeted you is my daughter, Valerie. And you're—"

"Roger Benedict."

Straightening abruptly, her blue eyes bright with pleasant surprise, Valerie stood holding a rain boot in each hand as she watched the two men shake hands over the counter. "Roger Benedict—the writer?" she asked.

The customer turned to Valerie. "Yes, young lady."

Valerie dropped the boots with a squishy thud and moved back around the counter, her face glowing with excitement. "Mr. Benedict, I loved your book on Colonial Williamsburg. And Enrico Romero's photographs were pure art!"

Now their customer regarded her quizzically. "You like Rico's work? I'll have to tell him that when I visit him later, at the hospital. It might amuse Romero to learn he has a pretty little fan in these parts."

Valerie frowned. The man's last remark rankled—along with the subtle dismissal that had crept into his tone. But curiosity won out, and she couldn't resist asking, "The hospital? Why is Mr. Romero in the hospital?"

"Actually, I was just going to tell your father all about that, if you'll excuse me," their visitor informed Valerie pointedly.

Valerie scowled to herself as the man turned away to address her father. This customer was something of a stuffed shirt, she thought, retreating behind the counter. Granted, he was older than she, but they were still both adults. He was treating her as if she were about seventeen years old!

Yet wasn't that how she looked, with her dishevelled hair, skintight jeans and clingy cotton T-shirt? Valerie chuckled to herself. When she'd left for her assignment earlier that afternoon, she had wisely resisted wearing good clothes out in the downpour. And by the time she'd arrived at the day-care center, her makeup had been so gooey that she'd wiped it off in the powder room. No wonder this man assumed she was below the age of consent. It might be interesting to set him straight.

Meanwhile she listened to him as he spoke to her father; he was wearing the same deep frown that had lined his face when he entered the shop. "I've brought in all of Rico's equipment, Mr. Vernon—mangled as it is. You see, we had a rather nasty accident yesterday, just outside your city. Some wom—I mean, some *person* rear-ended us royally, smashing most of Rico's equipment, not to mention breaking his shinbone."

"How terrible!" Valerie couldn't help but gasp from the sidelines.

Still seemingly oblivious to Valerie, the handsome stranger continued to her dad, "A pity, too, because Rico and I were on our way to Homochitto National Forest to finish my new book on warblers of the American South."

Despite herself, Valerie found her curiosity still getting the better of her. "Warbler? What's a warbler?" she asked their customer.

He turned to her, raising an eyebrow just slightly. "A warbler," he explained patiently, "is a bird."

Valerie gritted her teeth, feeling silly. "I mean, what kind of bird—"

"Species," he corrected rather irritably. "There are over sixty species of warblers."

With that, Benedict again turned back to her father. Valerie planted her hands on her hips and glowered her own annoyance. *Well, excu-u-use me*, she thought. Perhaps her inquiry about Enrico Romero had been a bit nosy, but it galled her that this man persisted in treating her as if she were a pesky child intruding on an important adult conversation. So what if he'd been around longer than she had; even if he was assuming she was a high schooler, that still didn't excuse his rudeness. And, recalling his frank appraisal when he first stepped into the shop, she could feel her irritation building. Obviously this man liked to feast his eyes on an attractive female—providing she kept her empty-headed thoughts to herself. What a chauvinist!

"What you can't repair," Benedict was now telling her father, "I'll want you to replace. Quite a nuisance, that wreck. Luckily, all my equipment was on the floor of the back seat, and the seat belt saved me from serious injury. But Rico—as usual—wasn't wearing his safety belt. He'll be laid up for the better part of a month and we're behind schedule, to boot. Damned inconvenient."

Appalled by the stranger's callousness, Valerie found herself speaking up. "But don't you care about Mr. Romero?"

The man again turned to her, this time glowering. "I beg your pardon?"

Though Roger Benedict's expression and his tone of voice were equally daunting, Valerie squared her shoulders and repeated, "I said, don't you care about Enrico Romero?"

"Meaning what?" he asked.

"Meaning that the man has a broken leg, yet all you care about is your—your bird book."

"*Warbler* book," he corrected tersely.

"Whatever. I am simply trying to point out that any normal person would be worried about—"

Their customer stiffened and shot Valerie a steely stare. "And what makes you think I'm not concerned about Rico? Or normal?"

Hearing her father's dry laughter in the background, Valerie continued to regard the frowning stranger. She had a sudden, sinking feeling that she was outmatched. "I just meant that your warbler project seems more important than—"

"You think it's not important to Rico?" he interjected. "And may I point out that none of my plans—or motives—are really any of your concern?"

Now Fred Vernon coughed and turned away to hide a rueful smile while Valerie instantly sobered, feeling rather foolish. Roger Benedict was right, she realized. None of this really was her business. And the man was a customer, after all. Whatever had possessed her to be rude to a customer—even one with a broad insufferable streak?

In the meantime Roger had already turned back to her father. "Now, Mr. Vernon, if you'll just have a look at the contents of Rico's case—"

But Fred Vernon silenced his customer by raising a hand. "Sorry, Mr. Benedict, I'd love to help you, but one of my best customers dropped off this camera during his lunch hour, and I promised him I'd get right on it." Smiling sheepishly at Valerie, he added, "Honey, would you mind helping Mr. Benedict?"

Valerie gritted her teeth, but managed to nod affirmatively to her father. She knew her dad was strapped for time, and vowed to serve Roger Benedict with a crisp efficiency, then send him on his way.

But Roger was already protesting to Valerie's father. "Perhaps I'd best come back when you're less busy, sir." Tossing Valerie a forbearing smile, he continued, "I mean, I'm sure the young lady is a perfectly competent clerk, but there's a lot of expensive, sophisticated equipment here."

That did it! Valerie glowered at Roger, her mouth poised to give this Neanderthal a piece of her mind. Luckily, before she could speak, her dad had already laid aside his tools and was facing Roger Benedict sternly. "I assure you that my daughter is just as capable of serving you as I am—probably more so."

"Really?" Roger looked highly skeptical. He turned to Valerie. "How long have you been working here, anyway?"

Valerie's father now chuckled again, and Valerie could have kicked him. Yet she managed to stare Roger straight in the eye and say with an air of boredom, "Oh, basically all my life— although I did have to take a sabbatical a few years back in order to get my degree in commercial photography."

"You did?" Roger muttered, looking rather taken aback.

Feeling a perverse satisfaction at his discomfiture, Valerie efficiently pulled the battered case in front of her. "Now how may this young lady help you—*Mr. Benedict, sir*?" In a voice dripping with sweet sarcasm, she added, "I do want to get this delightful little matter concluded so I won't be late for the sock hop tonight."

Now Roger looked very ill at ease, adjusting his glasses, while Fred Vernon again laughed off to the side. At last Roger turned to Valerie and said rather sheepishly, "Well, I'm afraid much of Rico's equipment is a total loss...."

For the next few minutes, Valerie helped Roger sort through the contents of the case. She uttered more than one gasp of dismay as she saw that he had spoken the truth; almost all of the top-of-the-line equipment was ruined.

"Why, there's thousands of dollars' worth of damage here!" she exclaimed, looking crestfallen as she pulled out a mutilated camera and two smashed telephoto lenses.

Roger nodded. "Rico's case was in the trunk, and received the full impact of the collision."

"It's a wonder you weren't hurt more," she murmured with a frown.

"Well, I do feel as if I've been hurled against a wall half a dozen times, but other than that, I'm really doing quite grand," Roger said dryly.

Valerie smiled at Roger's last comment, shaking her head as she continued to extract the mangled equipment from the case. As she and Roger discussed the loss together, some of the tension of earlier moments lessened, and she even noted a gleam of respect in his eyes as she described to him in detail the damage to each component, her expertise easy and fluid. Together, they divided the gadgets into two groups—those few that might be repairable, and the items beyond salvaging, which would be discarded after the insurance appraisal.

Their task nearly completed, Valerie felt a small twinge of disappointment that her contact with Roger Benedict was almost at an end. Though the man was a definite pain in the nether regions, she did feel intensely curious about him and his writing. Living in Natchez, she didn't get to meet many writers—certainly, she'd never met anyone who had collaborated with a famous photographer like Enrico Romero!

And face it, Valerie, she chided herself. *This man is handsome enough to be banned in Boston.* Older, distinguished, solid—she found everything about him appealing. His hair, now dry, fell in shiny, slightly wavy lines about his beautifully shaped head, as if to tempt a woman to touch the thick, silky texture. And his smile—when he deigned to use it!—was definitely an ice melter. He wore a very male, musky scent that mingled with an alluring natural essence, drawing her to him. All in all, Valerie had to admit that Roger Benedict exuded a potent male chemistry to which she was far from immune.

Realizing the traitorous path her thoughts were taking, Valerie felt her cheeks growing warm. She tried to cover her embarrassment as her fingers ineffectually struggled to close the latch on the now-empty aluminum case. But then Roger reached out to help her, and his hand brushed hers, sending an almost electric jolt through her body. She pulled her hand away, forcing a businesslike smile. Yet Roger's answering smile was more knowing, the sparkle in his deep-set eyes telling her he hadn't missed the effect his touch had on her. Mercy!

Their inventory completed, Valerie tried to maintain a matter-of-fact attitude as she made out the sales slip, writing down the address of Roger's hotel in Natchez, so they could later deliver the items to him.

As he prepared to leave, she couldn't resist asking, "By the way, you are a New Yorker, aren't you?"

"Yes," he replied, amiably enough.

"May I ask why you decided to drive all the way down here?"

"Migration," he answered.

"Migration? You mean you are going to move down here?"

He laughed, then said carefully, "During the springtime, birds migrate from south to north. Surely you studied this phenomenon in elementary school, Ms Vernon?"

Valerie mentally kicked herself. She had walked right into that one! But she managed to counter glibly, "Oh, yes, migration. I did study it in elementary school, and so recently. How could I have forgotten?"

Off to the side, Fred Vernon again laughed, shaking his balding head. "How long have you been watching birds, Mr. Benedict?"

Roger turned toward Fred, obviously warming to the subject. "Oh, for quite a few years now. Warblers are my specialty—in fact, writing this book is the realization of a lifelong dream."

"Birds have always seemed rather drab creatures to me," Valerie put in with a yawn.

Roger turned to her with a look of reproach. "Oh, but they're not drab creatures in the least, Ms Vernon. It's simply a matter of being observant of them in our environment." There was a hint of wry humor in his gaze as he stared at her intently and continued, "Consider, for instance, your eyes."

"My eyes?" she repeated, despite herself feeling a small thrill at his steady perusal.

He continued to study her in his direct, unnerving way. "Yes, Ms Vernon, your eyes. They're quite a startling shade of blue violet—but not nearly as striking as the indigo bunting in full plumage."

Issuing the double-edged remark, Roger turned to speak with Valerie's father again. She frowned, not at all pleased by his backhanded compliment. Valerie's eyes were her best feature, and this man had the gall to say they came in second behind some bird or other!

Fred Vernon was now handing Roger his coat and umbrella. "If there's anything else we can help you with while you're in Natchez, don't hesitate to call upon us."

"Thank you, sir." Shaking on his coat, Roger was turning to leave. But then he stopped in his tracks, snapping his fingers. Slowly pivoting to face Fred, he said, "There is one thing you might help me with, Mr. Vernon. Your sign out front includes a 'Vernon Photography.' Is that also you?"

Fred shook his head, proudly glancing toward Valerie. "My daughter."

Roger turned skeptically to Valerie. "You're a professional photographer?" Even as she indignantly opened her mouth, he held up a hand and said, "Right. Fine. I'd forgotten that you studied photography in college. Are you still active in the field?"

"Only when my father trusts me with his camera," she informed him with a saccharine smile. "I haven't thrown it in the toilet since I was in elementary school."

Now Roger was fighting a smile as he stared back at Valerie. "All right, Ms Vernon. Mea culpa. Now tell me, do you know of anyone in this area who is good—I mean, *really* good—at nature photography?"

At once Valerie was all attention. "You need a photographer?"

"I'll have to have someone else while Rico is laid up."

"You're not going to wait until he recovers?"

"I can't afford to. I'd miss my deadline."

By now Valerie's mind was humming. The man might be exasperating, but here was a professional opportunity she couldn't afford to pass up. Before she could lose her nerve, she said firmly, "Mr. Benedict, I'd be happy to offer my services."

"Oh?" He looked rather startled.

"As I mentioned earlier, I do have a degree in photography from Northeast Louisiana University, and my work has appeared in numerous periodicals in the area—"

"Including?" he asked with sudden interest.

She rattled off a half-dozen names of regional newspapers and magazines.

Now he was scowling again. After a moment, he shook his head and said, "I'm sorry, Ms Vernon. But I've never heard of any of those publications."

"Look, I'm good," she told him earnestly. "I'm sure I can provide you with whatever photographs you need for your book."

By now, Roger's brow was deeply furrowed, and he was obviously wavering. But after a moment, he again shook his head and said, "I appreciate your interest, Ms Vernon, but I'm afraid this book is just too important. I can't afford to take a chance on an unknown quantity."

"What if your first publisher had felt that way?" she asked indignantly.

He gave her an openhanded gesture. "You have a point, but I still need someone with more experience. I'm afraid I'm going to have to follow my original plan and call up some known names in the business."

Valerie was coldly silent.

Roger sighed. "Look, I really am sorry. No hard feelings, okay?" He glanced at his watch. "Well, if you'll excuse me..."

But as Roger again started to leave, Valerie felt compelled to rush after him. He gave her a bemused look as she caught up with him near the front door. "Yes?"

Though it went against the grain with Valerie to plead, she forced herself to give the writer an ingratiating smile. "Mr. Benedict, I don't mean to be a pest. But I know I can do the work you want, and do it well. My studio and custom lab are at the back of this shop, and if you'd just take a few minutes to study my portfolio—"

But he was already shaking his head. "Look, Ms Vernon, I didn't want to mention this before, but the truth is, my photographer will be spending six weeks alone working with me, in a small cabin out in the woods. Surely you can see how—" he paused to smile slightly as his eyes gave her a meaningful once-over "—unworkable and unwise that would be."

Valerie's cheeks burned. This man was unbelievable! "Why Mr. Benedict, I never would have expected to hear such a sexist remark coming from a supposedly sophisticated New Yorker like you!"

Roger glowered back at her from behind his glasses. "It wasn't a sexist remark, Ms Vernon. I'm simply recognizing the realities of the situation."

"Are you?" In her best imitation of a simpering Southern belle, Valerie added, "You mean that big, strong old you-all wouldn't be safe from little old me?"

"Apparently not," came his dry response.

Valerie threw up her hands. "I give up."

"Sorry," he repeated with a shrug as he once more turned for the door.

Valerie retreated to the counter, her face set in grim lines. Certainly she could understand Roger Benedict wanting a photographer with experience, but his dismissing her without even giving her a chance or looking at her work—that really galled her. And his chauvinistic crack about not wanting to take a woman alone to the woods had been the last straw. Watching her father finish loading the now-repaired camera, she was seized by a sudden, angry whim. She snatched up the camera, flipped on the strobe and pivoted to face Roger. "Smile!" she called out brightly.

Caught off guard, he turned to scowl at her even as she snapped the shutter. "Just a memento," she told him sweetly. "It's not every day that I meet a man who's so..." She paused to gesture extravagantly. "So liberal, so sensitive and open-minded, so willing to give a struggling fellow professional a chance."

For a moment, Roger continued to frown murderously at Valerie, his jaw clenched. He looked, startlingly enough, absolutely furious. Was it from her words or from her snapping his picture? she wondered.

Before she could contemplate these questions, Roger squared his shoulders with dignity, turned and, with a *whoosh* of rain from the opened door, disappeared into the bleakness outside.

"WOW! I'VE CAPTURED HIM!" Valerie cried, standing in her darkroom an hour later.

She held up the wet eight-by-ten glossy. Roger Benedict in all his glowering magnificence—the stern eyes behind the square-rimmed glasses, the straight no-nonsense nose, the tight, if somehow still sensual, mouth. And those dark brows, thunderously knitted. Very, very formidable. And very handsome.

She chuckled. She'd always assumed bird-watchers were skinny, knobby-kneed types who wore horn-rimmed glasses and pith helmets. But this bird-watcher was definitely no lame duck!

Valerie studied the photograph critically. Despite her hasty execution, the angle was good, the light excellent. Yes, it was one of her better shots—exposing all of Roger's dark, simmering hostility and displaying her talent as a photographer, as well.

Again she puzzled over Roger's angry reaction when she had snapped the shot. She had expected annoyance, but not the cold fury he had displayed when he stood rigidly at the door, directing a glare of laser intensity at her. She smiled to herself. It might be interesting to find out what made Roger Benedict tick, why he'd reacted with such rancor at having his picture shot.

As she clipped the photograph up to dry on a nylon line, her brain began to swirl in a thousand devious directions. Then, as a glorious idea crystallized, she clapped her hands in glee. Yes, she would do it! She wouldn't give up this easily!

Roger Benedict deserved it, anyway, for taking himself so damned seriously!

Leaving the darkroom, Valerie entered her small office and sat down at her desk. Grabbing the phone, she dialed the number of a local messenger service. "I need someone here in an hour," she instructed, "to deliver a photograph."

After the arrangements were made, Valerie rapped her pencil on top of her desk. What the devil was the name Roger Benedict had dropped? She grabbed the Natchez phone directory then punched out another number.

"Judge Armstrong Library."

"I need the name of a bird," Valerie began lamely. "An indigo bird..."

An hour later, Valerie sat at her desk, again staring at Roger's scowling face. All that remained was for her to write an inscription across the top of his raincoat.

She hesitated a moment, then chuckled, writing with style and flourish: "Bird's-eye view of Roger Benedict, famous species of American male chauvinist. From the Indigo Bunting."

2

"ARE YOU SURE you don't know of anyone else who might be available?" Roger Benedict barked into the phone, muttering an expletive under his breath.

Roger sat in his room at an elegant downtown Natchez hotel, a Scotch and soda in one hand, the phone at his ear. "Sorry, George," he went on sincerely after a moment. "I didn't mean to bite your head off. It's just that I've really been through the wringer the past couple of days, and my schedule has been blown all to hell. You're the last name on the list Rico gave me, and I'm at the end of my rope. I know I'm giving you short notice, and it's not surprising that you're tied up." He paused as George responded, then said, "Right. Call me back if you hear of anyone who might be available. Thanks, George."

Roger hung up the phone with a sigh and leaned back against the padded headboard of his bed, flexing his sore shoulder muscles. He was feeling every bit of his forty-five years tonight. Due to the wreck, his back and neck felt as if someone had been pounding him with a two-by-four. His body definitely wasn't bouncing back like it used to!

Roger picked up the photograph that lay next to him on the bed, and a grudging smile pulled at his mouth. What a glower, he thought, studying his face in stark, glossy black and white. Had he really been that much of a grouch this afternoon?

Yes, he had been damned irritable, and with cause, perhaps. He also hated having unauthorized photographs taken.

Yet Valerie Vernon couldn't have known that. The reasons had nothing to do with her, not really.

He scowled at the photograph again. She *was* good, and now he'd have to eat humble pie to get her.

Well, not too much humble pie. That just wasn't Roger Benedict's style.

He smiled ruefully as he recalled his moments with lovely young Valerie. He'd definitely gotten off on the wrong foot with her. Yes, he'd been out of sorts earlier today and not feeling too generous toward the opposite sex—not after that woman had totaled his car, had broken Rico's leg and then had the gall to insist that none of it was her fault. The woman had never even said she was sorry, despite the fact that Rico had been in excruciating pain, and this had infuriated Roger most of all. Then there'd been the hospital to take care of, police and insurance reports to fill out, not to mention worries about Rico . . . all of it a nightmare.

He sighed again. His mother had often accused him of being a perfectionist. Yes, he did like his life well-ordered. But since yesterday, a giant wrench had been thrown into the works of his smoothly running existence.

Then today, when he'd first seen Valerie in the camera shop, he'd assumed she was a nosy teenager, not the intelligent, inquisitive woman he'd later discovered her to be. Despite his sour humor at the time, he'd found her diverting. She was engagingly different from the women he was used to—spirited, unpretentious. And very attractive.

Very young. Nice long legs she had, glorious eyes—he'd teased her there, for her eyes did put the indigo bunting quite to shame!—and that mane of flaming auburn hair.

With her as his photographer for six weeks out in the woods, could he keep his mind on the birds? Despite himself, Roger chuckled.

Actually the pursuit of romance had not been a priority in Roger Benedict's life for some time now. He liked it that way—or so he often told himself. Ten years ago, Roger had endured a very bitter and very well publicized divorce, and for years thereafter, he'd been leery of becoming too heavily involved with the fairer sex. Then Claudia had come along. She'd been a botanist, writing a book on a grant. They'd met each other while doing committee work for the Audubon Society. They'd had a lot in common—both divorced, both interested in life sciences. They'd attended functions together, which had naturally led to weekend excursions and then longer trips. Eventually they'd moved in together. Their sex life had been fair, the companionship much better.

Then six months ago, Claudia had begun to move away from him emotionally. Within weeks she'd confronted the issue: "Roger, I've got to move out. I'm starting to see someone else, and I have a feeling it's going to get serious. Anyway, we've never lied to each other, and I don't want to start now."

Roger had taken the news like a man, respecting Claudia's honesty. In fact the two of them were still friends, even though she was now married to the professor she'd been seeing. In a way, Roger had been relieved that his relationship with Claudia had ended. Outwardly they'd been faithful to each other, and they'd both enjoyed the companionship, but on a gut level, the commitment, the love and the passion just hadn't been there between them.

Since Claudia had left, there'd been no one steady for Roger, only a few casual dates to social events he didn't want to miss.

And, frankly, at the moment, Roger Benedict was feeling damned sorry for himself. He knew he'd be stuck here at the hotel, alone, until he was sure Rico was settled in and recovering well. Monday, he'd need to arrange for a nurse to care for his friend until he could safely travel again. But in the meantime, Roger had the entire weekend just to stew, to think of how battered his middle-aged body felt and how far behind schedule he was getting.

At the moment, he could certainly use some feminine companionship. It didn't have to be anything sexual, just someone to pour his Scotch, rub his aching shoulders and say, "Poor Roger..."

Wasn't he deserving of that much?

Now Valerie Vernon would do quite nicely, he mused. He could just see her kneeling next to him in a black lace teddy, with those long legs of her, that riot of hair, and those compelling blue-violet eyes...

What was he thinking? Here, he'd just met the girl, she was almost young enough to be his daughter, and already he was practically seducing her in his mind! It had been some time since his libido had overridden his mature judgment this way, even in his thoughts.

But then, his libido had been sorely deprived for some time, he acknowledged to himself ruefully. And Valerie Vernon presented a mighty potent temptation—a temptation he would somehow manage to resist, for both their sakes.

Still he smiled. It was going to be an interesting six weeks, assuming he could now convince Valerie to accompany him to the forest. Tomorrow he'd swallow his pride and call her. Oh, he'd make her squirm a bit before he let her off the hook—he wouldn't be able to resist that after she'd sent him the photograph.

Yes, he'd make his move tomorrow. For now, he just wanted to have an early dinner, go check on Rico at the hospital then hit the sack early.

He placed the photograph on his nightstand. "I hope you know what you're getting yourself into, Ms Vernon," he murmured with an ironic smile.

Then he glanced at her inscription on the photo and frowned. On one point he'd definitely have to educate her. He was not a male chauvinist.

Well, not *that much* of a male chauvinist.

EARLY THE NEXT MORNING, the phone rang, jolting Valerie out of a deep slumber. Reaching for the receiver on her nightstand, she squinted at her clock, half-blinded by the sunshine streaming in through the window beside her bed. The dial read 8:00 a.m. On a Saturday morning, no less. Who the devil was calling her?

"Hello," she growled sleepily.

"Good morning, Ms Vernon."

It was him— Roger Benedict! His low, taunting voice was unmistakable. Instantly Valerie became alert

"Mr. Benedict?" she questioned, scowling at the phone.

"Correct. Don't tell me I woke you up, Ms Vernon?"

Valerie scooted up against her headboard, pulling a blue crazy quilt up about her. "Well, you might at least apologize for calling me in the middle of the night."

He chuckled. "The middle of the night? My, you are a sleepyhead, aren't you? I've been up for over two hours, spotting various species along your bayous here. I saw a blue heron and a yellow-billed cuckoo."

"Congratulations. I'm fascinated," Valerie said drolly. With scarcely veiled sarcasm, she went on, "It's a good thing you don't have a wife, Mr. Benedict." Frowning, she added, "Or do you?"

"Lamentably, no."

"Well, if you did, I doubt she'd appreciate being awakened before the birds on a Saturday morning."

"Doubtless, you're right," he concurred dryly. With a mock air of tragedy, he added, "I take it, then, that you're not volunteering for the job, Ms Vernon?"

"Certainly not." Yet by now, Valerie was grudgingly smiling, even as she heard him again laugh on the other end. Roger Benedict, the stuffed shirt himself, was actually flirting with her this morning. Hmmm, she thought. That meant he likely wanted something.

Abruptly he said, "Valerie I want to see you again."

"Oh?" she asked, her voice rising slightly.

"I want to take you out to dinner, get to know you," he continued silkily.

"I see," she murmured, her own controlled voice belying the fact that her heart was hammering and every ounce of her attention was riveted on the phone—as well as every molecule of suspicion she possessed! "And what is the purpose of this meeting, Mr. Benedict. Business or pleasure?"

His response was a dry chuckle. "That I prefer not to say."

"Then the answer is no," she said crisply.

She heard his low whistle. "Valerie, Valerie, don't you think you're being a bit shortsighted? You know, this could be the opportunity of a lifetime for you." After a meaningful pause, he added, "On the other hand, I could have some wicked sexist design on your lovely young person. So which will it be, Valerie? Are you willing to take the chance and go out with me? Or am I too much for you to handle?"

Now Valerie was glowering at the phone. Ever since hearing Roger's voice moments earlier, she had been waiting for his response to the photograph she'd sent him yesterday. Apparently he preferred a war of nerves to direct attack. It was quite obvious that the man was savoring some perverse, private glee in tormenting her. He was dangling the dinner invitation before her like a carrot, teasing and bemusing her. But he was too much of an insufferable male to admit that he really did need her professional services.

Well, in that case, he could take his job and . . .

She heard him sigh dramatically. "Well, Valerie, Lord knows I tried...."

"I'll go," she snapped. The words were out before she even thought.

Again she heard that maddening chuckle. "Splendid. Let's see, I've found your address in the phone directory—"

"That's right. But I live up—"

"And I'll call for you at seven."

The line clicked off.

VALERIE DRESSED in a khaki skirt, a navy blouse and brown leather sandals, then had her breakfast on her small private balcony overlooking the Vernons' lush backyard. She had enjoyed many a breakfast this way, ever since her senior year in high school, when her mother and father had converted their attic into Valerie's own studio apartment with private entrance. This was the Vernons' way of saying to their daughter, "We want you close, but we'll also respect your privacy." Valerie had left for college the next year, but the apartment and the Vernon house had remained her true home. As an only child, she felt a deep emotional bond with her parents. Following her mother's death in the past year, she had felt even more protective toward her father, staying on to help him out with his business.

And what sort of bond existed between her and Roger Benedict? She smiled at the thought as she sipped her orange juice. She did find Roger a very attractive older man—she couldn't deny that. She'd felt a surge of excitement—as well as no little amount of annoyance—when he'd teased her on the phone earlier that morning. She was definitely taking a risk in seeing him again. After all, he might have no intention of offering her a job; he could be planning simply to exact some sweet revenge due to the photograph she'd sent him.

She'd also have to inform her father of the date, because Roger had cut her off before she could explain to him that her apartment was situated above her dad's house. She remembered her father giving her a sideways, suspicious glance yesterday, when the boy from the messenger service dropped by for the photograph. Her dad had been very protective of her ever since her breakup with Mark, and she didn't know just how Fred Vernon would react to her seeing Roger tonight. Well, she would simply tell her dad that the meeting was strictly business. After all, wasn't there a fifty-fifty chance that she was right?

An optimistic estimate—to say the least!

Valerie frowned as she nibbled her French toast. She had to accept that in consenting to go out with Roger, she was risking another romantic entanglement. It had been a long time since any man had stirred her interest this way, not since . . .

She sighed, trying to distract herself by glancing down at the well-loved backyard of the Vernon home, forcing herself to concentrate on the massive oak tree standing squarely in the middle of the grassy area. Its gnarled branches stretched over toward the ground, the glossy leaves of its canopy reaching upward, almost touching Valerie's toes at the edge of her tiny veranda. A slight breeze was blowing, wafting the fragrance of jasmine over Valerie and rustling the leaves of the tree. The chirping of sparrows was soothing, as was the rattling of the rusty chains that suspended the old bench swing from the lofty oak.

The swing she sat on with Mark . . .

Distractedly she glanced at her watch. Thanks to Roger' wake-up call, she still had an hour before she was due at her dad's shop.

The old swing creaked remorselessly, bringing a lump to Valerie's throat. Despite her resolve not to think of her for mer fiancé, Valerie found herself remembernig the man who had turned her life topsy-turvy two-and-a-half years ago. She had met Mark Hastings at an oil rig near Laurel, Mississippi; as drilling supervisor at the site, he had assisted her on a photography assignment she'd gotten from an oil company technical journal. They were immediately attracted to each other, and a whirlwind romance had followed, with Mark driving from Laurel to Natchez to see Valerie each weekend. Within three months, they'd become engaged.

Things had turned sour soon after Mark's company went bankrupt during the oil industry downturn. Valerie had tried her best to be supportive, but Mark's male vanity had been badly burned by the loss of his job. He began to drink more, stood her up on dates, forgot her birthday and didn't call for ong stretches.

She began to suspect that he was cheating on her, although she had no solid proof. Finally the half-expected phone call had come, and Mark had been honest enough—or callous enough—to tell her the truth: he was marrying a girl from a wealthy Laurel family and had been invited into her father's lumber business.

Valerie bitterly recalled the time when her entire world had been shattered. She had felt so used, betrayed. To make matters even worse, soon after Mark deserted her, Valerie's mother became gravely ill. And much to Valerie's torment, Mark had called her several times after the breakup, claiming he still loved her and was miserable with his new wife. Valerie was invariably cold to him, yet still the calls continued....

The last call had come when Valerie's mother was in the hospital, shortly after the doctor told them she probably wouldn't be coming home this time. Valerie remembered clutching the telephone with trembling hands when Mark called; he had begged her to meet him.

It was then that Valerie made an important decision, growing up in that very instant. Mark was *never* going to hurt her again—no one would, ever! Her dad needed her, and she must be strong.

Calmly she had told Mark that if he ever called her again, she'd notify his wife. Then she had hung up the phone, swallowing her hurt. She hadn't heard from him since.

And she'd become strong, very strong. Her nerve endings had grown numb; her grief had been buried, raw, deep inside her, and she succumbed to it only in private moments. Even when her mother died, no one ever saw her shed a tear....

It had taken her a long time to get over Mark, but she'd done it. She'd concentrated on helping her dad and advancing her career. Yet now, for the first time in so long, another man threatened to make her feel again. It was exciting on one level, frightening on another.

Anyway, Roger Benedict was too old for her, wasn't he?

She wasn't sure. But she did know that Mark Hastings had been too young.

AT WORK, VALERIE WAS of little help to her dad. Though by now, she'd pushed aside her memories of Mark, her mind was still preoccupied by thoughts of the coming evening with Roger. She wanted this photography assignment so badly she could taste it! And the attraction she felt for Roger complicated things, keeping her thoughts in turmoil. Though she tried to keep her mind on her work, several customers had to repeat questions to her, and when she dropped a valuable lens, cracking it irreparably, she muttered a curse and chewed her bottom lip in exasperation.

That's when her father took her aside. "Val, what is it?"

Looking up at her father's lined, sympathetic face, Valerie knew she could no longer postpone telling her father about her planned meeting with Roger. She ended with, "Dad, this could be my big break."

But Fred Vernon was frowing at the news. "Valerie, don't tell me you're thinking of going off to the woods with that man to work on his book?"

"Dad, it's business," Valerie put in lamely.

"I don't like it," Fred said, shaking his head. "It just doesn't seem proper—the two of you alone there for weeks on end."

"Dad, I'm twenty-five," Valerie protested. "Don't you trust me?"

"Yes, I do. But I'm not so sure about this Roger Benedict character. Oh, he's a charmer, that one, but perhaps a bit too smooth and sure of himself."

Further discussion was postponed as two more customers came into the shop. They were quite busy for the balance of the morning. Yet when Valerie and her father closed down the store at two, Fred was still frowning. Valerie left quickly, determined not to allow her dad to talk her out of the meeting with Roger.

On an impulse, Valerie decided to buy a new outfit for the occasion. As she drove her small car toward a downtown dress shop she frequented, she questioned her sanity. Was she consciously trying to entice Roger?

Well, she rationalized, she did need to make a good impression if she intended to win this job. Roger wasn't taking her that seriously, and the right clothes would definitely help. She promised herself she'd purchase something very understated and professional.

Valerie parked in front of Myrna's Boutique. She left her car, taking deep breaths of crisp spring air as she approached the elegant old storefront. It was a clear, cool day. At least she wouldn't have to worry about getting drenched tonight.

Valerie swept through the curtained French door into the stylish interior of the boutique.

"Valerie!" came Myrna Floyd's bright greeting.

Valerie smiled as the pleasingly plump, graying woman came forward to give Valerie a motherly hug. "You got a big date tonight, honey? Need a pretty new dress?"

Valerie laughed. "Myrna, you're something of a mind reader. But actually, it's a business meeting."

Myrna gave Valerie a long look. "Is this meeting with a member of the male gender?"

"Well, yes, but—"

"Then it sounds like a date to me." Myrna took Valerie's arm, leading her toward a long, freestanding chrome rack. "I have just the thing for you, honey—just in from New York. When I saw that dress, I said to myself, 'Get Valerie Vernon in that creation, and she'll be snatched up by some handsome man before she can wink.'"

"Don't hold your breath, Myrna," Valerie rejoined with a chuckle.

"How's your dad doing, honey?" Myrna asked as she moved aside a black bombazine cocktail dress.

"He's adjusting fine, thank you," Valerie replied with a half smile. Myrna, a widow, was a long-standing friend of the Vernon family and a member of their church. For many years the astute shopkeeper had provided the women of Natchez with stylish fashions at very reasonable prices. Though Myrna's question about Fred Vernon had been casual, the intent gleam in her warm brown eyes had told Valerie that her interest in Fred Vernon was more than just friendly. This pleased Valerie to a degree, since Myrna was delightful and would make a good companion for her father. Yet Valerie also wasn't sure she was quite ready to let another woman take her mother's place in her father's heart.

"I know the dress is on this rack somewhere," Myrna was mumbling, plowing through luscious silks and crepes. "And I'm delighted that you're my first customer today, Val. We'll find the dress and have a nice chat while you try it on."

The phone rang, and Myrna turned from the rack, sighing as she flashed Valerie an apologetic smile. "Sorry, honey, you'll have to hunt for it yourself. I'll be right back." As she hurried off toward the counter, she called over her shoulder, "It's a flowered silk print with a three-tiered skirt."

A three-tiered skirt indeed, Valerie thought as she turned to the rack of dresses. Actually she was relieved that Myrna had been called away; the shopkeeper seemed intent on dressing her up like a floral arrangement. Dismissing the rack of dresses after a brief, fruitless perusal, Valerie turned to a nearby rack of suits, searching for the image of elegance and professionalism. She selected a stylish linen suit with a yellow-gold jacket, black pleated skirt and coordinating printed blouse. She headed unobtrusively for the dressing room, noting with relief that Myrna was involved in a lengthy, agitated conversation regarding a supplier's late delivery.

Inside the tiny mirrored dressing room, Valerie removed her blouse and skirt and donned the suit. It fit perfectly, and she glanced with approval at the image she projected—just the right mixture of chic and professional elegance. At home she'd add matching pumps and purse to complete her ideal of the well-dressed businesswoman.

Looking up, she frowned slightly. Her hair, falling in thick auburn waves about her shoulders, was her only remaining concession to girlishness. She gathered her heavy tresses in her hands, pulling her hair away from her face to effect a knot at the back of her head. Yes, that was the look she wanted. Restrained, sophisticated.

"Oh, no, honey."

Valerie turned to face Myrna, who stood at the curtained doorway with arms akimbo, her round face puckered in a frown.

Myrna entered the tiny room, clucking at Valerie. "No way, honey. You look like you're on your way to meet with the IRS. Take it off."

"Myrna!" Valerie's hands were on her hips now, her lips twisted in a half smile of amusement mixed with annoyance.

"I'm not selling that suit to you, Val, and that's final," Myrna countered vehemently.

With these words, Myrna turned and exited the room, pulling the curtain closed behind her and leaving Valerie to scowl as she tapped her foot in exasperation.

But then Myrna reentered the dressing room, carrying a vividly patterned cocktail dress, and Valerie's heart melted.

"Perfect, isn't it?" the older woman inquired, smiling as she held up the dress for Valerie's scrutiny.

"Oh, Myrna," Valerie breathed, her gaze fastened upon the creation. The dress was indeed exquisite, and Valerie couldn't resist taking it and holding it in front of her. The fabric was mouth watering, a tightly controlled collection of flowers in vibrant shades of orange, yellow, lavender, pink and bright sapphire blue. The style was sleeveless with a low, rounded neckline. It was fitted to the hips, where it flounced out in three tiers, with the hemline just above knee level.

"Dare I look at the price tag?" Valerie whispered to Myrna.

"No, just put it on," the older woman directed.

Valerie found she couldn't resist. Afterward she stared at herself in the mirror. Myrna had been right—the dress looked great on her, hugging her willowy torso and showing off her legs. But . . . She eyed the dress's daring décolletage, which revealed a generous portion of her firm breasts. "This design certainly leaves little to the imagination."

"That's the idea," the older woman replied coyly. "Just look how that flowered print complements the creamy tone of your skin, and the high hemline is perfect for long legs like yours. Honey, with your body, you should be a model."

Despite herself, Valerie smiled. "I happen to prefer the other side of the camera," she quipped. She dared a glance at the price tag. "Oh, Myrna, this dress would cost me half a week's salary."

Myrna shrugged. "Give me a deposit today and the rest when you have it."

"That's not it, Myrna. I have the money, and I'm sure the dress is worth every dime. But it's just that it seems so darn frivolous—"

"How old are you, honey—twenty-five? And already talking like a crotchety old spinster, I see. What's a child like you supposed to do but be frivolous?"

Valerie stared at her reflection for a long moment. She bit her lip. "Well, I do have some high-heeled sandals that would be perfect with this—"

"That's the spirit!"

"Sure, what the heck?" Valerie echoed, caught up in Myrna's excitement despite herself. Staring at her reflection again, she added, "Well, kid, kiss your paycheck goodbye!"

THAT EVENING AT SEVEN-THIRTY, Valerie was pacing her apartment in a swirl of vividly patterned skirts. It was seven-thirty, and Roger was late! Unkind thoughts raced through her brain as to what he might be up to. Perhaps he was simply planning to stand her up as punishment for the photograph.

More tense moments passed, and Valerie continued to pace. Her apartment had never looked better, and normally she would have paused to glance approvingly about the pastel-toned studio and kitchen, at the rooms tastefully dec-

orated with white rattan furniture, huge comfortable throw
pillows and a few delicate French Provincial pieces. Yet at the
moment, Valerie could not have felt more agitated if the entire apartment were painted crimson. And the only object in
the room that commanded her attention was the clock—
which now read twenty to eight!

By a quarter to eight, Valerie decided that enough was
enough. When and if Roger Benedict arrived, she refused to
be here waiting for him like some starry-eyed groupie.

She grabbed her bag and headed for the door, only to stop
in her tracks when she opened it.

Roger Benedict stood on her balcony with hand poised to
knock, looking dazzlingly handsome in a tan tropical wool
suit, white dress shirt and tan-and-gold-striped silk tie. His
other hand held an eye-catching bouquet of flowers, mostly
roses and carnations. The luscious shades of pink, yellow and
rose looked as if they'd been plucked straight from her dress!

His dark gaze flicked over her approvingly, then he
dropped his hand to his side. He whistled low under his
breath and said, "Good evening, Valerie. So kind of you to
spare my knuckles."

Valerie was tempted to glower at him, but his show of
humor made it difficult, and she merely stared back at him,
feeling at a loss.

After a moment, he cleared his throat and inquired dryly,
"Aren't you going to ask me in?"

She found her voice. "Of course. You're only—" she
glanced at her watch "—forty-five minutes late."

Chuckling, Roger swept past her through the open door,
and the smell of him wafted over her—the enticing, musky
essence of his cologne, mingled with a vague aroma of whis-
key. Once she had followed and had shut the door, he turned
to give her a gesture of supplication. "Valerie, my lateness is

not my fault. I arrived promptly at seven, but your dad shanghaied me, insisting that I have a highball with him, while he grilled me on my life history and future plans."

"Oh, brother." Valerie groaned.

"It seems you forgot to tell me that you live above your dad's house," he chided, still grinning.

"You hung up on me this morning before I could give you that information," she pointed out ungraciously.

He shrugged. "Whatever. I did assure your father that my intentions toward his precious daughter are strictly honorable, and that I'll have you home before dawn—" he paused to wink at her solemnly "—on Monday."

Valerie paled. "You didn't!"

"You're right, I didn't," Roger rejoined with a grin. "I know a concerned father when I see one. Not that I blame your dad in the least." Looking her over again, he added, "If you were mine, I'd feel exactly the same way."

Roger's last words and the meaningful look in his eyes sent a shiver down Valerie's spine. There was a certain underlying seductiveness in the words, "If you were mine." He hadn't said, "If you were my daughter," or, "If you were my sister," but "If you were mine." Realizing that Roger was still staring at her, Valerie cleared her throat and said, "Dad just doesn't understand that this is business. Um—you did tell him that tonight's meeting is business, didn't you?"

"Ah, yes, I did tell him that," Roger rejoined. But his tone was teasing, and there was now a devilish sparkle in his eyes.

"Oh, you're exasperating!" Valerie said, blushing and fighting a smile despite herself. Roger could be a charming scoundrel when he wanted to. And as much as her father's overprotective behavior miffed her, she also couldn't help but feel somewhat amused by Fred Vernon's typical shenanigans.

Roger took a step closer to her. "You do look lovely to-night, Valerie," he breathed, a husky catch in his voice. His gaze moved slowly over her again—studying her dress, her face, then lingering on her hair, which she'd worn down in loose curls about her neck and shoulders. The flush that seconds earlier had highlighted only her cheeks now threatened to suffuse her entire body. As Roger's brown gaze moved downward slightly to lock with hers, he extended the bouquet. "For you. Let's call it a small peace offering."

Valerie didn't know quite how to react to Roger's sincere statement or the appreciative gleam in his eyes. With trembling fingers, she took the bouquet. "Thanks, Mr. Benedict. They're lovely."

"Please—won't you call me Roger?"

"Very well, Roger. Just let me put these in water."

She went off to her small kitchen and soon emerged with a tall glass vase half-filled with water. She began arranging the flowers on the dining room table, and Roger came over to join her. "The flowers match your dress," he said. "And that's some luscious creation you're wearing."

"Thank you."

He was moving even closer to her now, his nearness continuing to unsettle her. "You know, you'd look quite alluring with a carnation right here, behind your ear." He pointed out the spot with his hand, and she struggled not to shudder as his fingertips grazed her earlobe. "Why not put a blossom or two there?"

It was on the tip of her tongue to retort, *Because I don't want to allure you*, but then she realized that such a remark would be unwise and probably dishonest. So instead she grinned at him and quipped, "Because I'd look like a tropical drink."

"I agree—delicious." He stepped even closer, his male scent making her senses swim as he reached out and broke off a pink carnation from her bouquet. "You know, Valerie, as a writer, I lay out my settings in great detail, and tonight, I see you with flowers in your hair." He stuck the flower behind her right ear, then winked at her again.

"Really? Which book did *that* line come from?"

He chuckled. "And here I thought I had you completely psyched." Glancing at his watch, he added, "Well—shall we go?"

Finished with the flower arrangement, she hesitated. "Roger, before we go—"

"Yes?"

"Won't you take a few moments to study my portfolio? It's just over here on the coffee table—" Her voice trailed off as she started toward the suede-covered album on the rattan table.

He followed her. "That won't be necessary, Valerie."

She turned to him sharply. "Meaning that this evening is to have nothing to do with business, after all?"

"That's not what I said," he pointed out. "The fact of the matter is that I've already seen your work."

Valerie felt herself blushing again. "But that was just one photograph."

He smiled. "Let's just say your one picture was worth a thousand words."

"But—"

"Come on, Valerie," he said impatiently. Spotting her evening purse on the coffee table, he grabbed it and stuffed it into her hand. "If we don't leave right this minute, we'll miss our dinner reservation."

He tugged her toward the door. Outside, as they started down the dark stairs, his arm slid protectively about her waist, and she found his nearness quite stirring in the balmy sweetness of the night. "Mind telling me where we're going?"

"Ms Vernon, we're going on a dinner cruise aboard the *Delta Princess*."

3

NIGHT HAD DESCENDED by the time they reached the landing, at the base of historic Silver Street in Natchez-Under-the-Hill. Valerie held Roger's hand as they moved toward the boarding ramp in the scant light. The April evening was pleasantly cool and clear, a thousand stars winking to life in the vast heavens. Above them to the east rose Natchez's famed bluff, a steep rise covered by kudzu vine, its hungry tendrils curling upward to climb the shadowy shapes of trees atop the hill. Behind them, along Silver Street, sounds of revelry spilled forth in the restored restaurant and bar district. And ahead of them towered the majestic *Delta Princess*, a gleaming, three-tiered light festival, cradled by the mighty Mississippi, beckoning them with the romantic swell of string music and the tantalizing aroma of Creole food.

All her life, Valerie had occasionally glimpsed the old-time riverboats traveling the wide Mississippi, taking their passengers into the life-style of another age. But seeing the majestic white *Delta Princess* at close range was a special thrill for her now.

Roger held her hand tightly as they ascended the steep plank to the main deck of the stern-wheeler. As the boat's steam whistle blew, billowing white smoke into the cloudless sky, Valerie felt transported into another age—indeed, into a fantasy filled with wonder and magic, not the least of which was the handsome man at her side.

On board they were greeted by the captain, a tall middle-aged man wearing an immaculate brass-buttoned white uni-

form. "Good evening, Mr. Benedict. I'm delighted to welcome you and your lovely companion on board tonight."

Roger introduced Valerie to the captain, then said, "Captain Miller, I must again thank you for your kindness in allowing us along for the dinner excursion this evening."

The other man smiled. "It was a pleasure to meet you in
person this afternoon, sir. And with several of our passengers staying over in Natchez for the weekend, we certainly
have ample table space available tonight."

The captain led them around the deck to the bow entrance
of the main cabin. As they stepped through the open French
doors into the long, narrow hall, Valerie smiled, feeling captivated. The scene that greeted her did seem from another
time. Brightly dressed people sat on comfortable captain's
chairs around linen-draped tables, while white-uniformed
stewards moved soundlessly on the lavender-and-rose patterned rug, carrying trays laden with luscious food and drink.
The string quartet was beginning a lovely rendition of "Night
and Day."

Captain Miller seated them near the bow end of the hall.
Valerie looked around approvingly. From their position, they
could hear and see the string quartet and had a good view,
through the open French doors, of couples moving outside
to dance on deck, in the moonlight-strewn shadows.

Valerie was entranced. Her eyes sparkled as she again heard
the steamboat's whistle and felt a gentle rocking motion.

"You should see your face!" Roger said with a laugh.

Valerie turned to him excitedly; she had almost forgotten
her companion in her fascination with the steamboat. "We're
moving, aren't we?"

Again he chuckled. "Don't tell me you've never been on a
steamboat? Not you—a resident of historic old Natchez?"

"Well, my parents did take me on some excursion boats
when I was a child, but never on a big stern-wheeler like this
one." She leaned forward and asked Roger, "You mean that

today, you just walked up to the captain and asked him if we could come on board tonight?"

He laughed. "Count on a native to know nothing of the goings-on in the area. Besides, the steamboat was docked here for the weekend. Why shouldn't they let us on board?"

Valerie was shaking her head, her eyes gleaming with new respect for Roger. "No wonder you've been so successful in writing your travel books." Looking about again, she added, "It never would have occurred to me to ask."

Roger continued to eat up her unabashed reaction. "You know, Valerie, you're very fresh. Very spontaneous. I like that."

Taken aback by his unexpected and sincere compliment, Valerie was staring at him blankly when the steward came up to take their drink order. The young man informed them that the string quartet was playing a tribute to Frank Sinatra's music tonight. In the moments that followed, Valerie and Roger chatted over frozen daiquiris and enjoyed the music. She grilled him about some of the books he'd written, and he told her of his adventures in exotic locales such as Hong Kong and Majorca. Moments later the steward returned to offer them choices for the evening's fare.

"I saw Rico today," Roger remarked after they had ordered.

"Oh? How is he doing?" Valerie felt a twinge of guilt that she hadn't thought more about the ailing photographer since yesterday.

"The wreck shook him up pretty badly, but he's doing remarkably well under the circumstances," Roger replied. "In fact, the doctors are letting him loose on crutches tomorrow. I'm sure the fair belles of Natchez shall rue the day."

Valerie couldn't resist teasing, "Shades of the pot calling the kettle black?"

Roger gave her a look of mock reproach as the steward brought their first course of shrimp remoulade on a heavy bed of lettuce. As they began to eat the deliciously spicy dish, Roger flashed her a charming smile and said, "Rico may come out to see us at the cabin in a few weeks."

Valerie almost choked on her lettuce. "Us?"

Roger chuckled. "Yes, us, Valerie. I'll keep you in suspense no longer. I want to take you under wing."

"Under wing?" Valerie repeated blankly.

"I want to hire you as my photographer. Are you interested?"

"Interested?" She could barely contain the surge of excitement consuming her. "Why yes, of course. I accept."

He grinned. "Splendid."

Then reaction set in for Valerie. Roger's sudden turnabout was almost too good to be true. "Tell me, Roger, what prompted your offer? You've not seen my work."

He slanted her a stern glance. "As I pointed out earlier, I have seen your work. And besides," he admitted sheepishly, "let's just say I owe you one."

"I beg your pardon?"

He gave her an openhanded gesture. "All right, I'll admit it. Yesterday when I met you, I was an asinine grouch. After the wreck, my body felt as if it had been through a cement mixer. Plus the woman who rear-ended us never even apologized and showed no concern for Rico's injuries. I guess that experience left me not feeling too kindly disposed toward the fairer sex."

"I see," Valerie murmured, feeling warmed that Roger was lowering his guard enough to share such an honest insight with her.

"Anyway," he was continuing, "yesterday, when I met you, I'll admit I didn't take you that seriously, not until you sent me the photograph. You see, at the photography shop, you looked about seventeen years old, and you just seemed to be such—"

"A woman?" she finished.

He scowled. "Look, Valerie. With the type of writing I do, I'm continually hounded by amateur photographers, of both sexes. So of course I have to be somewhat skeptical."

"Okay," she conceded, "perhaps you do. But do you deny that you would have preferred to hire a man for this assignment?"

"I don't deny it. And I believe I've already outlined my reasons there."

Valerie stared him straight in the eye. "I've told you I can handle that."

Surprisingly he laughed, then murmured, "Maybe it's not you that I'm so worried about."

Valerie stared at him, her cheeks growing warm. His provocative words hung between them like a live electric current. After a moment, she managed to tear her gaze from his and wisely returned her attention to the food.

As they began eating redfish smothered in piquant Creole sauce and drinking champagne, Valerie frowned thoughtfully and ventured, "A moment ago you spoke of wanting to take me under wing. Would you mind explaining that to me?"

He smiled. "I think it's pretty obvious."

"Is it?"

He leaned forward slightly. "There's much I can teach you—about photographing birds, and about getting ahead in the publishing business. You're helping me out in a pinch, so I think it behooves me to do what I can to help you advance your career."

Valerie was pleasantly surprised. "I see. That's generous of you, Roger."

He shook his head and smiled. "Oh, don't make me out to be too noble. I'll certainly benefit from our arrangement. And I must also warn you up front that Rico will likely be finishing the book, not you."

Valerie started to protest, then thought better of the idea. After all, it *was* Rico who had been hired initially; it was only fair that he be allowed to finish the book.

"Though Rico may be back in business within a month," Roger was continuing, "I wish to hire you for the entire six weeks. If Rico recovers before then—" he paused, smiling "—we'll find something for you to do."

"Is this the standard do-you-type-and-fix-coffee speech?"

He raised a finely shaped eyebrow. "Why Ms Vernon! Would I stoop to making such a sexist remark?"

"Yes," she replied, her blue eyes gleaming victoriously, and they both laughed.

They ate in companionable silence for a few moments, then Roger put down his fork and said thoughtfully, "Tell me something, Valerie. If you truly want to succeed as a commercial photographer, what are you doing living in Natchez, Mississippi?"

Valerie replied carefully, "After college, I did think of moving to New York and seeing if I could free-lance for some of the big magazines. But about that time, my mother became ill, and my dad needed my help with his business. When Mom died a year ago . . ." She bit her lip, then continued, "Well, I couldn't leave my father alone so soon after . . . Anyway, I suppose that eventually I'll have to make the break."

Roger was again looking at her in that keenly perceptive way of his that was so unsettling. "You know you're remarkable. I like loyalty and old-fashioned values."

Valerie stared up at him, far too affected by the deep sincerity lighting his brown eyes. "You do?"

He laughed and shook his head. "Valerie, you're a delight."

Their dessert had now arrived, luscious pecan pie. As they ate the sinfully rich concoction and drank generously brandied *café brûlot*, Roger inquired, "So how many birds have you photographed?"

Taken aback, Valerie thought about the question a moment. "Well, in college, we did all kinds of nature photography, studying many animals, including birds. And lately—" She scowled, then said, "why just last week, I did the charity cat show in Jackson."

"Cats? Good Lord, not cats."

Valerie giggled. "Cats—and birds," she murmured. Of course, cats would have to be any bird-watcher's nightmare. Whatever had possessed her to make such a ridiculous statement? Was the champagne going to her head? Trying to sound confident and glib, she continued, "Anyway, I'm sure I'll be able to handle this assignment just fine."

"Let's hope so," Roger concurred dryly. "At any rate, I am at your mercy, since no one else was available."

"So that's it!" Valerie gave him a cool stare. "No wonder you've been oozing charm tonight."

"Have I?" he asked innocently.

"You have. Pretty desperate, weren't you?"

He smiled tightly. "Of course I had to check to see if someone more experienced was available. While your belief in your talents is commendable, I think you're going to find that photographing warblers is hardly a waltz in slow time. Rico has always said that capturing lightning on a tree branch is much easier. But since you seem to be doubting my esteem for your talents, let me explain the financial arrangements to you."

Valerie cooled down as Roger explained his offer in detail. The terms were quite generous. When he finished, he politely waited for her response.

"Very well, so I'm hired," she said. Leaning forward, she added, "But I'm curious about something. Why did you keep me in suspense for so long? Thirty seconds on the phone this morning would have sufficed."

He smiled sheepishly. "Well, actually, you're right. But if I'd told you on the phone this morning, you wouldn't have come out to dinner with me tonight, and actually..." His voice trailed off and he glanced about the salon, loosening his tie. At last he said in a rush, "Well, to tell you the truth, Valerie, I've been feeling rather sorry for myself, stuck here all weekend, with Rico laid up..."

Valerie smiled. Roger had a penchant toward the melodramatic that was rather endearing. She answered his stab at martyrdom in her best Southern belle simper. "Why, you poor dear. Now what can we do to make big old you-all feel right at home?"

He chuckled, then drawled back, "Well, you could dance with me, Ms Vernon."

Before Valerie could even think of protesting, Roger stood and helped her to her feet. She let him lead her outside to the moonlight-strewn deck. He took her into his arms, leading her about expertly as the quartet launched into a new, poignant selection Valerie could not quite recognize.

Swirling in Roger's strong arms, Valerie felt a wave of exhilaration. She had the job, her goal for the evening was accomplished! The night was gorgeous and clear, the breeze caressed her face, and Roger's warm hand at her back sent delicious shivers down her spine. She let herself relax and just enjoyed the music and being in Roger's arms.

But while Valerie was feeling exultant, Roger was already beginning to regret his hasty impulse to ask her to dance. Ever since he'd picked her up two hours ago, he hadn't been able to keep his eyes off her. Valerie Vernon was pure seductress in that frothy, vibrant silk dress she was wearing, her thick auburn hair falling in tantalizing waves about her lovely face and neck. Besides being sinfully beautiful, the girl was also a marvelous conversationalist; indeed, her company had fascinated him on every level. A moment ago, she'd just looked so delightfully impish when she'd feigned her Southern belle simper and had asked what she could do to please him. Before he knew what was happening, he'd pulled her to her feet and had hauled her out here—straight into very dangerous territory. Now she was in his arms—slim, warm, sexy—and driving him insane!

And knowing that he shouldn't be feeling this way about a girl this young did nothing to diminish his frustration—or his desire for her.

"What's that song?" she murmured, breaking into his tense thoughts.

"I beg your pardon?" he asked rather stiffly.

"The song the string quartet is playing. I can't quite recognize it."

Roger listened to the selection a moment, then groaned, muttering the title under his breath.

"I'm sorry, I didn't understand you," Valerie said patiently. "Can you repeat—"

"'I've Got You Under My Skin,'" he said.

"Oh." She laughed rather nervously. "Gee, that's good, Roger. It's a real oldie, isn't it?"

He harrumphed. "One wouldn't expect a child your age to be a connoisseur of Cole Porter."

Valerie stiffened slightly, frowning up at him. "Hey, what's this, Roger? Are you mad at me now?"

He shot her a dark look. "Not in the least."

"I thought we were getting along so well, and that we had everything settled."

"We do," he said tersely.

"Then why are you angry at me?"

"I'm not the least bit angry," he snapped back. "And why should I be, anyway?" *Just because you're the sexiest little siren I've ever held in my arms* . . . he added to himself ruefully.

"Well, I don't know," she said defensively. "But you sure sound hot under the collar to me."

No lie, he thought to himself, without answering her.

Just then, another couple glided dangerously near them, and Roger pulled Valerie close to prevent a collision. Staring up at him and absorbing the tense, smoldering look in his eyes, she shivered slightly.

"Damn, you're cold, aren't you?" he muttered with a confusing tenderness.

Roger pulled her even closer and tucked her head beneath his chin, his hand moving upward to warm the gooseflesh on her bare upper arm. As much as his behavior baffled her, Valerie realized she was approaching shaky ground. Her face was pressed against the hollow of his throat; her senses were absorbing the masculine essence of his skin. He felt so good, so male and strong, as he led her about. The moonlight and his nearness created a potent mixture in her veins, and if she had ever wondered whether this man presented a very real temptation, she didn't doubt it now.

"You shouldn't have worn this skimpy little dress," he scolded after a moment, a telltale huskiness in his voice. "It's almost as bad as your skimpy little jeans yesterday."

She laughed and pulled back slightly. "Aha! I knew you were looking yesterday!"

"Damn right," he replied self-righteously, fighting a smile. "What do you expect a man to do when he sees the likes of you in skintight jeans? Actually, I was rather relieved to learn that you weren't seventeen years old, so I didn't have to feel like such a lecherous old reprobate." His arms tightened and his tone grew tense as he added, "Then you took that blasted photograph."

"I knew you were still mad about it."

"Do you know what I wanted to do when I received it?"

"Please, don't tell me," Valerie replied with a small shiver. "I can well imagine."

"Can you?" Just then the music stopped, and Valerie pulled away from him. She tottered slightly as the boat moved.

Roger stared down at her with a debilitating intensity in his eyes. "Did you imagine this, Valerie?" he whispered.

Slowly, so slowly she thought she was dying, he drew her closer again, and his lips descended on hers. Valerie was so caught up in the magic of the evening, in *his* magic, that she couldn't have resisted him if the boat had caught on fire. At first his lips were experimental, tasting her, then he groaned and kissed her with deepening hunger. His tongue parted her lips, stealing inside her mouth and savoring the sweetness within, and she shuddered, reeling from the hot, electrifying invasion. He crushed her closer then, making her breasts throb from the hard pressure of his chest.

Valerie curled her arms around Roger's neck and surrendered to his kiss. Oh, she had forgotten how it felt to be held and kissed like this—to be afire with the taste and feel of a passionate lover. Indeed, to be honest, she had never been kissed like this—not even by Mark! Roger's cologne and the natural smell of him were a tantalizing opiate for her senses, and the rhythmic pressure of his tongue deep in her mouth was driving her insane, sending hot rivers of excitement rushing down her body, until a fierce need for him settled in the womanly center of her, making her ravenous for the ultimate fulfillment she knew this man could bring her.

Valerie was reeling, pressing herself eagerly into Roger, when abruptly he released her and moved away. He strode over to the railing and stood there with his broad back to her. Watching him, Valerie fought a sudden tear, her lips still throbbing from his kiss. Roger had taken her into his arms and had stripped her bare emotionally, and then, just as quickly, he had rejected her. What was wrong with him tonight, anyway? Was he angry at her again? Had she disappointed him? Or what?

After a moment, she squared her shoulders and walked over to join him at the railing. They stood there for a long, tense moment, both staring out at the water, the silence between them electric. Behind them, the other couples were returning to the salon, and for the moment, the only sound was the muffled plodding of the boat's paddle wheel.

Roger was gripping the railing and shaking his head. "Why did I do that?" he asked no one in particular.

"I beg your pardon?"

He turned to her with an apologetic smile. "I'm sorry, Valerie. I didn't intend for that to happen just now. Too much champagne, I guess."

Valerie felt her spine stiffening. "Too much champagne?" she repeated. "Obviously, then, it couldn't have been me."

He laughed ironically but didn't answer her. After a moment, he sighed and said, "Oh, Valerie. I think we have a problem."

"Do we?" she asked. She wasn't at all pleased to hear Roger refer to their kiss as a "problem."

Another tense silence settled between them. Finally Roger turned to her and said, "Valerie, let's face it. You were right. It wasn't just the champagne. We're attracted to each other. I feel it. You feel it. Can you deny it?"

"No," she said in a small voice.

"And I'm afraid—well, that what we're feeling could interfere with business."

She glanced at him sharply. "Are you withdrawing your offer?"

"No. I'm just afraid this attraction could complicate things."

"Not if we both behave like professionals," Valerie pointed out firmly. "We'll just have to keep things separate and put business first."

"Do you really think that will work?" he asked.

"Why shouldn't it?"

He caught an uneven breath. "Because I'm afraid we're going to be spending the next six weeks fighting—" he paused to look her over meaningfully "—a very powerful magnetism."

Despite a dizzying surge in her senses at Roger's words, his look, Valerie steadied herself and faced him bravely. "Look, I've already told you that I can handle this if you can."

"That's not the message I got when you were in my arms just now."

"Then what are you saying?" she asked in a voice filled with both frustration and uncertainty.

He stared out at the river, frowning deeply. "I'm just saying that—" His voice trailed off, then he groaned his frustration. "I don't need you doing this to me right now."

Now Valerie's pride was ruffled. "What's *that* crack supposed to mean?"

He shot her a dark look. "I think it's pretty obvious."

"Then I must be quite dense. Please explain it to me."

He looked her over again, his meaning blatant in his eyes. "Your dress. Your hair. You figure it out."

Valerie was seething. "Wait just a minute, Roger Benedict! You sound like I programmed this whole little scene tonight. Who flirted with me on the phone this morning? Who plied me with champagne, then danced with me in the moonlight?"

"All right, all right, I'm guilty, too," Roger said passionately. He stepped closer to her, sighing. "Look, Valerie, I'm just trying to warn you that what I would want from you—well, wouldn't be so nice."

"I beg your pardon?" she asked, her voice rising.

"I'm trying to tell you there's no future in it."

Valerie was flabbergasted and infuriated. "And just when did I ask for a future with you, Mr. Benedict?"

He spoke with strained patience. "Valerie, you're young and idealistic. I know the kinds of things a woman your age dreams about—the cottage with the white picket fence, the station wagon full of kids—all those things. I'm just saying that I've reached a stage in life where I have far more realistic expectations. I can't fulfill your dreams for you."

"Fine," she snapped back. "I don't want any of those things from you, anyway—believe it or not. So why are we having this conversation?"

For a moment, neither spoke as they confronted each other in the darkness. Then Roger moved even closer, taking Valerie's chin in his hand. Despite her anger, the intense look in his eyes riveted her to the spot as he whispered, "I'm just trying to warn you to be careful, darling. A man can only withstand so much temptation. I just might try to take you on in more ways than one."

Now Valerie burned from head to toe—especially where Roger had touched her. Flinging off his hand, she retorted, "Why of all the arrogant, conceited . . . What do you think I'm going to do, anyway, throw myself at you?"

"Well, no, I—"

"Was your kiss just now your insurance that I'll help you complete your precious little project?" she continued with furious sarcasm. "Don't tell me you're suggesting bedroom privileges as a part of our bargain?"

"Of course I'm not suggesting that," he said tightly.

"Good. Because that's one aspect I'd never agree to. So I'm glad we're getting the ground rules straight now." She tilted her chin and stared at him defiantly. "When do we leave for the woods, Mr. Benedict?"

"You still want to go through with this?"

"I wouldn't miss it for the world," she practically spat out.

He sighed. "Very well, then. We leave on Tuesday." They continued to glare at each other in the charged silence as the steamboat began making a slow circle in order to head back for Natchez. Then Roger ran a hand through his hair and said, "I apologize if I spoke rather crudely just now. I was only trying to be honest with you. That was some very powerful chemistry that flared between us. I just don't want things to, well, get out of hand."

As much as Roger aroused her with his provocative statement, his male presumptions maddened her more. "Don't hold your breath, Mr. Benedict," she informed him tersely, if in a voice that trembled. "At the risk of crushing your rather substantial ego, I must say that I think I can manage to resist you. You see, for me, there has to be a lot more to a caring relationship than just chemistry." Pointedly she added, "I'm afraid you greatly overestimate your charms."

Roger was opening his mouth to reply when Valerie abruptly swung about and walked back into the salon. He followed her, scowling.

LATER, SAFELY AT HOME, Valerie was still seething as she recalled her moments with Roger on the deck of the *Delta Princess*. She'd felt so moved by their kiss, so drawn to Roger, only to have him dismiss the episode as little more than lust—and dismiss her as little more than a child! The gall of the man, insinuating that she wanted a future with the likes of him. Here she had hoped Roger was different, yet tonight he'd demonstrated that he was too much like so many other men—just another male on the prowl, looking for a fling.

Well, he was looking in the wrong place! She'd be damned if she'd become just another feather in Roger Benedict's pith helmet. If he thought he was taking her off to some lurid little love nest, he had another think coming! At any rate, she did have the assignment now, and she would handle it like a professional.

At last Valerie collapsed on her bed and realized she was trembling quite badly. She was so confused. The truth was, Roger's kiss had curled her toes, and as furious as she'd been at him out on deck, when he'd called her "darling," she'd practically dissolved at his feet.

How could she feel so hurt, so angry at him, and still want him so much?

BACK AT HIS HOTEL, ROGER was also brooding as he got ready for bed, chastising himself for his conduct with Valerie. Was he succumbing to some crazy middle-aged urge to recapture his youth?

Valerie had been right tonight. It hadn't been just the champagne. He had been flirting with her all evening.

Hell, he'd been flirting with the girl from the moment he'd laid eyes on her. Valerie's beauty, her fresh, spontaneous qualities, had delighted him. And from the moment he'd seen her tonight, he'd been playing with fire—and getting burned. All his good intentions—indeed, his self-control—had flown out the window.

When his control had finally snapped, when he'd taken her in his arms and had kissed her, the taste of her had been as delicious and warm and exciting as everything else about her. The only reason she wasn't in his bed right now was the painful realization that his bed was all he truly could offer her. They had no real basis for building anything beyond that, and she was too fine a girl to be used in that way.

He groaned. Why was it that when he finally found a woman he was attracted to so genuinely, she was all wrong for him—too young, so far removed from him in so many ways? Valerie hadn't liked him much when he'd laid things on the line so bluntly tonight. Indeed, he'd intensely disliked himself when he'd stood there and deliberately diminished himself in her eyes.

Yet he had felt he owed her fair warning. He had his life in order now. If he ever made a romantic commitment again, it would have to be with a more mature woman who wanted the same things from life that he did at this stage of the game. He was in no shape to take on a bright-eyed, bushy-tailed twenty-five-year-old whom he could never keep up with. He didn't need this sweet young thing getting under his skin.

Yet Valerie was there, nevertheless. Even as he later went to bed, he found himself unaccountably humming, "'I've Got You Under My Skin.'"

4

"GOOD MORNING, VALERIE."

Valerie clutched the telephone receiver in a half daze, blinking at the near-blinding sunlight streaming down upon her bed through the sheer panels behind her. A glance at the bedside clock confirmed her worst suspicions—8:00 a.m., again! After a near-sleepless night!

"Don't you ever sleep?" she growled to Roger Benedict, her voice hoarse with sleepiness and sarcasm.

"Why, Valerie, I'm starting to worry about you," he replied with maddening self-possession. "Surely you don't think I'll allow you to laze about in bed all morning once we're out in the woods?"

Valerie felt her face burning at his gibe. "May I remind you, Mr. Benedict, that I'm not officially in your employ until Tuesday? After that, if you want me up with the birds, then that's exactly what you'll get."

He chuckled. "I'm quite reassured, Ms Vernon."

"And in the meantime—"

"Yes?"

"I'd appreciate your allowing me to get some much-needed rest."

He whistled. "My, aren't we touchy this morning. And you haven't even asked me why I've called."

She gritted her teeth. "Why have you called?"

"I'm inviting you to have lunch with me and Rico. Since you'll be taking over his duties, I thought a meeting would be in order."

"Oh," Valerie muttered. "Then Mr. Romero is out of the hospital?"

"He will be, as of ten o'clock this morning. I just have to get him checked out and settled in his new quarters. My hotel manager recommended a bed-and-breakfast here off Homochitto Street."

"I see. Are you sure he'll feel up to going out?"

Roger laughed. "Rico's already called me twice this morning to complain about the hospital food and to ask when I'm going to spring him loose. So how about it, Valerie? Have lunch with us?"

"Fine. I'd be delighted to have lunch with Mr. Romero," she replied pointedly.

There was a moment of silence, then Roger asked, "Twelve-thirty, then?"

"One o'clock. I have to attend church first with my dad."

"Then we'll pick you up at one. In the meantime, why don't you get some more sleep, sunshine?"

Valerie rolled her eyes as Roger clicked off. Of course, after hearing his voice, getting further rest was impossible.

VALERIE FIXED HERSELF some Belgian waffles in the microwave, and after she ate, she dressed in a pale blue cotton knit dress with matching jacket. The dress was one of her favorites; it had a pleasing rounded neckline, and it hugged her slim figure nicely without venturing into impropriety. She revived her mussed coiffure with the hairbrush and curling iron, then applied a light coating of makeup and lipstick. She hesitated a moment, then reached for a crystal bottle, dabbing on a few drops of her favorite perfume.

Staring at her reflection in the medicine cabinet mirror, she had to admit that she was taking special pains with her appearance again, as she had last night. And this, she acknowledged, was what just one kiss in the moonlight had done to her—even though Roger Benedict had acted like a jerk afterward. She still seethed every time she remembered him flaunting his romantic prowess to her and insinuating that she wouldn't be able to keep her hands off him once they were alone out in the woods.

Yet despite her resentments, Valerie couldn't hide that she was excited about seeing Roger again. He was nothing if not a sexy, challenging man. However, she would do her damnedest to hide these feelings from him!

She looked herself over again and was pleased by what she saw. Oh, well, she thought with a certain vindictive pleasure, let Roger see what he was passing up. At any rate, she would get to meet Rico Romero—a world-famous photographer she'd admired for ages—and this was ample reason to look her best. She'd already resolved that she would take along her portfolio and hoped that Rico would ask to see some of her work.

An hour later, Valerie was in her dad's car, heading for their church. Across from her, Fred Vernon was silent as he steered the car down the shady streets in the sweetness of the April morning.

Valerie knew her dad was curious about her meeting with Roger the previous night, even though he hadn't questioned her directly. She decided that she may as well dive in and tell him her plans. There was precious little time left before she'd be leaving with Roger, anyway.

"Dad," she began carefully, "I wanted to let you know that last night—well, Mr. Benedict offered me the photography assignment and I've accepted it."

Fred's expression was grim as he braked for a light. "I see." He tossed his daughter an admonishing glance. "You know how I feel about you going off with that man, don't you, honey?"

Valerie tilted her chin slightly. "Yes, Dad, I do."

Fred sighed. "I wish you'd reconsider."

"I can't," Valerie said earnestly. "I understand your misgivings, but I can't pass up the assignment. This opportunity is too important to my career."

Her father was scowling deeply as he accelerated the car. "I never thought I'd see you going to these lengths to get ahead," he muttered under his breath.

Valerie felt stung. "Just what is that comment supposed to mean? Do you honestly think I'd agree to an arrangement with Mr. Benedict that—that went beyond business?"

Fred glanced at her, his expression troubled yet conciliatory. "Of course not. Your mom and I raised you to have solid values, and I'm not questioning those now. I know you'd never intentionally get pulled into an involvement that—well, wasn't right for you. But I'm not so sure about this Roger Benedict character. I don't want to see you getting hurt and used again."

Valerie stiffened her spine. "I've grown up a lot since Mark and I broke up."

"I know you have, honey," her father concurred sympathetically. "But you've still got to be careful. Going off to the woods with a man like Roger Benedict is a provocative situation, to say the least. Like I told you yesterday, he's a little too slick, a bit too smooth an operator for my taste. And he's quite a bit older than you, too."

Valerie rolled her eyes. "I'm an adult and perfectly capable of taking care of myself."

Fred harrumphed. "A man like Roger Benedict probably has half a dozen girls like you for breakfast—"

"Dad, be serious!"

"I *am* being serious."

"Oh, for heaven's sake! I'll only be gone for six weeks."

"A lot can happen in six weeks," Fred pointed out grimly.

Valerie turned away to hide a sudden, perturbed frown. A lot could indeed happen in six weeks, she realized. A lot could happen in a single evening spent alone with Roger Benedict!

AT ONE-THIRTY, VALERIE was with Roger and Rico Romero at a fashionable restaurant out on the bluff. The Victorian decor was airy, and the location of their table near a window provided an enchanting view of tall trees in a tangled ravine plunging down to the Mississippi.

The three had been chatting casually as they drank white wine, ate shrimp cocktail and perused the menu. Valerie found Rico Romero to be good-looking and quite a charmer. Even with the cumbersome cast on one leg, he was still a force to reckon with—lean, dark haired, dark eyed, with classically handsome features. The other evidence of his and Roger's accident—a scattering of bruises on his face and a thin cut along one cheekbone—only added to his male appeal. He looked to be in his late twenties and was evidently something of a ladies' man, if the teasing coming from Roger's quarter was any indication.

While the two men had been indulging in good-natured ribbing ever since they'd picked up Valerie, Roger had acted rather reserved around her. When he'd come to her door to get her, his eyes had slid over her quite thoroughly. Yet he'd made no comment on her appearance; indeed, he'd acted politely detached and businesslike as he ushered her downstairs, helped her into his car and introduced her to Rico.

Now, as she studied the menu, she glanced at Roger and found he looked very handsome and rather intimidating as he stared at his own menu. The room was bright, fully illuminating the streaks of silver in his dark hair and the lines on his handsome, tanned face. Roger's maturity made him much more appealing to her than Rico Romero. And seeing Roger's broad hands on the menu, Valerie couldn't help but remember him touching her so provocatively last night. Studying his sensual male mouth, she couldn't help but recall their kiss....

Valerie realized she was staring at him quite boldly even as he glanced up at her sharply, raising an eyebrow. Luckily, at that point, the waitress walked up. "Well, what can we get for you folks today?" the middle-aged woman asked with a smile.

"What will you have, Valerie?" Roger asked.

"Oh, I think the spinach crepes," she replied smoothly.

Roger ordered Shrimp Creole, while Rico requested a big bowl of gumbo. After the waitress left, Valerie asked Rico, "So, Rico, are you happy to be out of the hospital?"

"Am I ever!" he replied, his dark eyes sparkling. Winking at her confidentially, he added, "My nurse looked like Attila the Hun, and every time I tried to get out of my bed, she threatened to sit on me."

As Valerie laughed, Roger coughed and said forbearingly, "May I add that Rico totally defied his doctor's orders the entire time he was hospitalized. And I really feel quite sorry for his poor nurse—who looked nothing like Attila the Hun, by the way."

"And the food," Rico went on disparagingly, ignoring Roger. "Why, they didn't even have a wine list."

Valerie shook her head as Roger harrumphed and said, "I rest my case."

Touching Rico's arm, Valerie asked, "Are you sure you're up to being out with us today?"

"I wouldn't have missed it for the world," Rico assured her. "One more dish of Jell-O or cup of chicken broth and I would have gagged." Grinning at Valerie, he added, "Besides, I just love the company."

She felt herself blushing and drew away her hand. She glanced at Roger, only to find him scowling at them both.

As they ate their delightfully spicy Creole and Cajun entrées, Rico asked Valerie, "Hey, as Roger and I were driving over to pick you up, I noticed several ladies in hoop skirts on the steps of the mansions we passed. Is everyone here still living in the last century?"

Valerie laughed. "To a degree, we are. Actually, what's going on right now is the annual Natchez Spring Pilgrimage—it's a festival to showcase the many antebellum mansions here."

Rico's dark eyes lit up, and Valerie realized that in many ways, he was still a kid. "Gee, that's fascinating. How many antebellum homes do you have here?"

"We have over five hundred antebellum structures still standing. It's really the largest collection in the South."

Rico whistled, then turned to Roger and said, "Hey, Roger, let's do the tourist thing this afternoon—you, me and Valerie."

Roger scowled at Rico as he set down his fork. "Have you lost your mind, Romero? Your doctor has prescribed *very limited* activities for the next few days. And just what were you planning to do if any of the homes don't have wheelchair access?"

"Wheelchair access," Rico repeated ruefully, eyeing his cast. He shrugged to Valerie. "That Roger. Such an old fogey. No sense of adventure."

Valerie giggled, but when she chanced a look at Roger, she found him still scowling at her and Rico.

"All Roger really cares about is birds," Rico was continuing drolly.

"Is that right?" Valerie asked him, rather pleased to observe through the corner of her eye that Roger now looked downright formidable, his brow deeply furrowed as he glowered at her and Rico.

"I'm afraid so," Rico answered confidentially. "You know, one time I had dinner with Roger and half a dozen of his bird-watching cronies. All they did was crack jokes about their little adventures in the woods. And I was the only one there who didn't understand why any of it was funny."

Valerie raised her napkin to cover a smile and avoided Roger's eye.

"Now if it were me, going to the woods with a woman like you . . ." Rico was continuing, his dark eyes sweeping over Valerie meaningfully. He grinned. "Well, you wouldn't need a crystal ball to know where my mind would be. But as for good old Roger—"

"Yes?" Valerie inquired, her lips twitching.

Rico leaned toward her. "All I can say is that if a bear comes stalking you, you'd better pray that there are no warblers warbling about."

"All right, Romero, that's enough," Roger put in tersely.

"Oh, but it's true," Rico went on to Valerie. "Heaven help you if Roger should spot that Beckman's whatever it is—"

"Bachman's warbler," Roger corrected testily.

"Roger has been trying to spot that bird for ten years," Rico told Valerie. "I'm beginning to think it's just an illusion—a flight of fancy, so to speak."

"Oh, the Bachman's is real, all right," Roger informed them rather imperiously. "And actually, I have an excellent chance of spotting it in the Homochitto National Forest at this time of year. It's been spotted there several times before."

Rico rolled his eyes at Valerie. "See, what did I tell you? A fanatic."

Valerie glanced at Roger, offering him a sheepish smile, but he was still frowning.

As they were finishing their meal, Rico nodded toward the folder at Valerie's feet. "I see you've brought along your portfolio. May I see your work?"

"Of course—I'd be delighted," Valerie replied with a brave smile.

Rico spent long moments studying Valerie's photos, then glanced up at her and said earnestly, "These are good, Valerie. Really good." As she beamed ecstatically, he turned to

Roger, holding up one of her black-and-white eight-by-tens. "Just look how she has captured the light in this shot, Roger."

Roger studied Valerie's striking photo of a barge floating down the Mississippi at sunset. "I agree," he told Rico with a stiff smile. "Valerie's work is excellent."

Rico had brought along his own portfolio, and soon he brought it out to show Valerie pictures of some of the birds he and Roger had spotted and photographed on the way down from New York. His work was impeccable, but he accepted Valerie's lavish compliments with surprising modesty. "I've never done much nature photography before," he confessed to her. "But Roger convinced me that we shouldn't break up the team, since we've collaborated successfully on several books already." Smiling at her warmly, he added, "I'm really relieved that you're going to be filling in for me, considering the tight deadline Roger and I are facing. Your work is fine, but I do pity you having to photograph warblers. It's exquisite frustration."

Valerie and Rico continued to discuss technical aspects of the project, while Roger sipped his coffee and listened. Several times Valerie tried to pull Roger into the conversation, but he resisted. Finally she gave up and just enjoyed visiting with Rico. If Roger was determined to be terse and uncommunicative today, that was his problem. At any rate, she was relieved and happy to learn that Rico evidently felt no resentment toward her for taking over his duties. She'd been especially thrilled to learn that he liked her work.

After lunch they drove Rico about town a bit to appease his desire to see some of the mansions, and he took a number of photographs from the car. At five o'clock, when the two men dropped Valerie off, Rico waited in the car while Roger escorted her to her door. The two arrived at her upstairs stoop in awkward silence.

Valerie ventured a shy smile at Roger. "Thanks for th lunch."

"You're welcome," he replied, adjusting his glasses. "You seemed to enjoy yourself today."

She bit her lip, uncertain what he meant. "Yes, I did."

"A pity Rico's leg is broken, or I would have asked him to escort you upstairs," he continued sarcastically. "You two *youngsters* really seemed to hit it off."

Her eyes narrowed. "Hey, hold on there, Roger. I'm not the one who was ribbing you."

"You laughed," he pointed out tersely.

"Rico was funny."

Roger harrumphed. "Rico's a flirt."

"I didn't think he was a flirt."

"Maybe you're a flirt, too."

Valerie was incredulous. "Now wait just a minute, Roger Benedict," she said, fuming. "Just because I found Rico friendly and entertaining—"

"And I wasn't, I presume?"

"No, as a matter of fact, you weren't. You were rather surly and rude all afternoon." Suspiciously she added, "And why are you discussing this with me now, anyway? Actually, you've said more to me in the last minute than you've said all day."

His scowl deepened. "I suppose you're right. We don't do a very good job of talking to each other, do we?"

"No, we don't." For a moment, they merely glared at each other in the charged silence, then Valerie sighed explosively and added, "Since you obviously don't enjoy talking to me—or being in my company—why are you still hanging around?"

He smiled slightly and moved closer, his dark eyes roving over her intimately. There was a trace of huskiness in his voice as he said, "Oh, I never said I didn't enjoy your company, Valerie. I just think it's pretty obvious that talking is not what we do best."

Exasperated, she said, "Then what—"

Given the tension between them, Valerie was stunned when Roger abruptly said, "God, you look lovely today," stepped closer and caught her beneath the arms. Her purse and keys rattled to the stoop, and she gasped in helpless anticipation as his dark eyes blazed down into hers and his mouth descended.

Roger's kiss was passionate, demanding, and Valerie was at once as aroused as she was surprised. At first she was stiff in his embrace, but then he whispered, "Kiss me back." His sexy words and warm lips turned her to mush, and she opened her mouth wide to him, curling her arms around his neck and absorbing the wonderful male smell of him as their tongues clashed in passionate interplay. His fingers flicked over her breasts, stroking provocatively, then he dug his hands into her hips and hauled her closer. She whimpered in mindless pleasure. He felt so solid, so strong, so crushingly, deliciously male against her. She realized poignantly that his distance today had actually hurt her, and this was the cure she needed, they both needed.

"Do you know I've wanted to do this all day?" he asked, kissing her cheek, her hair, then her neck. "Do you know...?"

His mouth passionately drank of hers again, his body pressed her against the door, and from deep in her throat came a muffled sigh of surrender....

But as abruptly as his kiss began, it ended. Without a word of explanation, Roger released her, picked up her purse and keys and stuffed them into her hands. Before she could even react, he turned and strode off down the stairs.

Watching him desert her, Valerie was trembling with hurt and confusion, her feelings in an uproar from his kiss. "No again!" she cried to herself through gritted teeth. Throwing down her purse and keys, she called after him angrily. "Roger! Damn it, you can't just kiss me like that then walk away!"

He paused at the bottom of the stairs to smile up at her tightly. "I'll pick you up on Tuesday. Six a.m."

"Six a.m.?" she repeated with bewilderment.
But he was already disappearing around the corner.

Returning to his car, Roger was shaking his head and mentally kicking himself. "At your age," he groaned.

5

It was still dark on Tuesday morning when they pulled out of Natchez. As Roger's rented car glided over the rolling, tree-lined terrain east of the city, Valerie, seated next to him, could hardly believe she had gotten ready on time.

She was still half-groggy, after staying up packing much of the night, and she was thankful that Roger had been quiet since he'd picked her up twenty minutes earlier. Stretching her jean-clad legs, Valerie remembered Roger telling her goodbye on Sunday. She'd been flabbergasted by his abrupt announcement that they would be leaving for the woods before dawn today—especially since his curt words had come mere seconds after he'd again kissed her so passionately.

Now she eyed him covertly and found he looked quite the rugged outdoorsman this morning, dressed in a plaid flannel shirt, jeans and brown leather hiking boots. But his face, as he watched the road, was impassive, and she wondered if he was still angry at her, as he'd been on Sunday. He'd seemed almost jealous then, yet he'd blown hot one minute, cold the next. If he truly was jealous, then how could he have just walked off and left her at her door—after that very torrid kiss, no less?

The man was definitely hard to figure out, but she was beginning to suspect that Roger Benedict had a sadistic streak. This leaving town at six in the morning, for instance. The forest was only an hour's drive, so what was the big rush? Roger had to have known that she would have a hectic time getting off, and perhaps this pleased him in some perverse way.

She'd had a devil of a time trying to decide what to bring. Would they, for instance, need dishes, pots, linens? These questions had plagued her, and she had almost called Roger, but then she'd decided to heck with it. She'd packed for herself, including her own linens and a sleeping bag, resolving that if Roger forgot cooking supplies, that was his problem. Besides, a man would never call up Roger and ask him what to bring, nor would a man show up carrying everything but the kitchen sink!

Valerie grinned, remembering his grudging smile when he'd picked her up and had discovered she carried only one suitcase, a duffel bag with her bedroll and her photography equipment. It was a good thing she had packed sparingly; the car was stuffed with his equipment, luggage and boxes of kitchen supplies.

Valerie may have packed light, but she was also prepared for any contingency. She felt herself blushing slightly as she remembered breaking down yesterday and packing her diaphragm. Was she consciously planning to go to bed with Roger out in the woods?

No, she wasn't. But she did know that after Sunday, she'd be a fool if she didn't prepare herself. She was nothing if not a realist.

While her feelings were certainly at war where Roger was concerned, she still broke out in shivers every time she remembered him holding her on Sunday, his mouth so deeply locked on hers. The softer, more passionate side of her nature kept arguing that surely it wouldn't be a crime to go further with this. They were both adults, and they were both so obviously attracted to each other. After all, she was a young, healthy woman who had been deprived of sex for some time, a woman who was going to be alone with a virile, dynamic man. Granted, one minute she wanted to strangle Roger for his arrogance, but the next . . . well, if he came on to her *that* strong again, she'd best have her bases covered!

"Any trouble getting off, Valerie?" he now asked, breaking into her thoughts.

"Oh, no," she said stiffly.

"Have everything you need?"

She turned toward the window to hide a new, very hot blush. "Yes."

"I found Rico a nurse yesterday," he went on conversationally. "An LVN."

"Oh, you did? Does this one look like Attila the Hun?"

He chuckled. "Not at all. In fact, she's a very beautiful—and very engaging—young Cajun. Poor thing, she'll have her hands full with Romero, although I assume he'll want to fly back to New York once he's getting around better."

"I hope he'll be feeling better soon," Valerie put in sincerely. "I saw him wince a few times on Sunday, much as he tried to hide his pain."

"You're very observant," Roger said. "And by the way, after our meeting with Rico on Sunday, he told me that it's fine with him if you want to finish up this entire project."

Valerie laughed in pleasant surprise. "He did? Gee, that was generous of him."

"I think Romero was quite impressed by you and your work," Roger said rather tightly. "And, bizarre as this may sound, I really think he wants to take it easy for a while."

"He should," she said.

The conversation lagged for a moment, then Roger cleared his throat and said, "Valerie, I've been wondering about something."

"Yes?"

"How does your dad feel about you going off with me like this?"

She sighed. "I won't lie to you. He's not pleased."

"But still you came."

She nodded. "Yes, I came. I realize that sooner or later, I may have to leave Natchez permanently. Taking school pictures and passport photos, along with occasional assignments for regional magazines, is hardly my idea of a lucrative photography career. Still, it's hard being away from Dad. This is the longest I'll have left him alone since Mom died."

"You're a very devoted daughter."

"Well, I've got a wonderful dad to be devoted to." She brightened a bit. "Actually, I feel a little better about it all since I called Myrna Floyd yesterday." At Roger's curious glance, she explained, "Myrna's an old friend of the family, and I think she has her sights set on Dad."

"I see you frowning when you say that."

"Well, it is kind of hard. Mom hasn't been gone that long. But I feel better knowing that Myrna will be checking in on Dad while I'm gone."

They fell into a comfortable silence. Valerie blinked as a needle of sunlight threaded its way through the trees along the road, piercing the windshield to shine directly into her eyes. As her vision adjusted to the light, she watched spellbound as the sun rose over the tops of the lofty pines ahead of them. Gradually the entire landscape was illuminated with golden light, revealing deep green loblolly pines, towering magnolias, and dogwood bedecked with luscious white blossoms.

"It's awe inspiring," Valerie breathed to Roger.

"Worth getting out of bed for at 5:00 a.m.?"

"Bed? What's a bed?" she quipped. Smiling at Roger, she added, "I've been meaning to ask why you chose Mississippi as the setting for your warbler book, anyway."

"It's not really the setting, per se, since I've been compiling data on warblers for years, during several trips to the South. However, due to spring migration, there is a very high density of many species of birds in Mississippi right now, including most Southern varieties of warblers. There's really no better location for the conclusion of my research, as well as the taking of photographs." His face lit up as he continued, "Also, a friend of mine from the Audubon Society spotted a Bachman's warbler nesting in this area last spring. That's the species Rico mentioned on Sunday—the one that has eluded me for ten years. I consider spotting and photographing the Bachman's almost critical to my book. And we don't have a lot of time," he added. "The manuscript is due in ten weeks."

"I see," Valerie murmured. "You really do love birds, don't you?"

He nodded. "I find them very graceful and lovely creatures." Smiling at her, he added, "Have you ever watched an eagle dive for a fish? First he soars, then he spots the fish and drops toward the water. In a split second, he snatches the fish with his talons, then he sails off. It's the most breathtaking sight I've ever witnessed."

"I'm sure it is," Valerie concurred, impressed by his sincerity. "Tell me, what prompted your interest in all of this—birds, the outdoors?"

Surprisingly Roger frowned at her question. "Actually, I suppose my interest in nature sprang from my childhood, when I spent most of my summers at camp in Colorado. You see, I come from one of those families who believe children should be seen and not heard—thus it was boarding school in the winter, camp in the summer."

"I see," Valerie replied, sensing the bitterness behind Roger's words. "How sad. You must have grown up feeling like an orphan. Were you an only child?"

"Yes."

"You, too," she said with a smile. "Then we have something in common, although my childhood was obviously quite different from yours. To think that your parents missed all the joys of raising you—"

His laugh cut short her words. "Oh, my parents were hardly domestic types. They were gone traveling in Europe a lot—often separately. Actually, I was far closer to my grandparents."

"Then I'm glad you had your grandparents, at least. So what did you do when you came of age?"

"Well, after prep school, I went on to Yale, then started my writing career, and then—"

"Yes?"

Roger took a deep breath, then said, "I'm divorced, Valerie."

She felt taken aback. "You are?"

He nodded. "It's been ten years now."

"Oh."

He glanced at her awkwardly. "Do you want to hear about it?"

"Sure, if you don't mind talking about it."

He paused a moment to gather his thoughts, then said, "Catherine was also from an old New York family. It was a happy marriage at first, but eventually we realized that we just didn't share the same interests. She was involved with the ballet and the Whitney Art Museum, I was involved with the Audubon Society and the Museum of Natural History. I wanted children, she didn't. She didn't like traveling with me, and we just kept drifting further apart. However, when the divorce came, it was surprisingly bitter."

"It was?"

He nodded. "Catherine wanted the house I'd inherited from my grandparents out on Long Island, even though she was quite wealthy in her own right and I'd offered her a generous cash settlement. Anyway, I wasn't willing to give her my house—some of my fondest childhood memories occurred there."

"I don't blame you," Valerie said. It endeared Roger to her to learn that his reasons for wanting to keep his house were sentimental, not material.

"I wish Catherine had been as reasonable," he said bitterly. "As it was, our court days were highly sensational, since Catherine's family was quite prominent in New York politics." Gripping the steering wheel, he added, "Photographers kept showing up, taking unauthorized photographs—"

"So that's why you resented my taking your picture last week!"

He smiled tightly. "I'll admit that I wasn't thrilled."

"I must apologize, Roger," she said lamely. "I just didn't know—"

"Of course not. You were far too busy savoring your own sadistic delight in tormenting me."

She glanced at him uncertainly. While he'd made his resentment of unauthorized photographs obvious, he'd also laced his last statement with a touch of humor, and somehow, she knew she'd been forgiven. "So—did you get to keep your house?" she asked him.

"I did. And Catherine hasn't spoken to me to this day."

Valerie shook her head. "I'm sorry, Roger. That must have been rough. Then you've been alone ten years now?"

He hesitated a moment, then said, "Actually, there was someone else for a number of years afterward. We were companions as much as anything else. When that relationship ended, at least the parting wasn't bitter."

Valerie nodded sympathetically. "I know what you're talking about. You see, I got burned once. It's tough to get over."

He frowned as he glanced at her. "Want to tell me about it?"

Valerie bit her lip, wavering. She was tempted to tell Roger about Mark; he seemed surprisingly human this morning.

The fact that he was confiding in her about his past love life made her wonder if he wasn't wrestling with the same temptations that she was. Or, he could be trying to tell her in his subtle way that romance was not something that had worked well for him in his life. Finally she said, "Would you mind if I take a rain check on that? I mean—it hasn't been that long for me."

"Still hung up on the guy?" Roger asked with a frown.

"No," Valerie responded quickly. Turning away, she added in a small voice, "To be honest, still a little hurt, I guess."

Roger's scowl deepened as he realized that the mere thought of a man hurting Valerie made him very, very angry.

NEAR THE FOREST, they stopped for groceries at Broussard's, a store on the highway not far from the town of Meadville. The establishment was a typical general store, boasting everything from groceries and clothing to hardware and sporting goods. Valerie loved the smell of the place—the leather, beef jerky, spices and freshly baked bread.

"You folks headed for Clear Springs Recreation Area?" the proprietress inquired.

Valerie placed the last of her purchases—a pound of butter, a carton of eggs and a quart of milk—on the countertop. Roger had asked her to buy the perishable items they'd need while he gassed up the car. "We'll be staying at the national forest, yes," Valerie replied, smiling at the tall, gray-haired woman standing across from her. "Are you familiar with the area?"

The woman waved a long, slim hand at Valerie. "Familiar? Lived here all my life, honey. How long you folks staying, anyhow?"

Staring at the woman's warm, lined face, Valerie could not be irritated by her inquisitiveness. "Six weeks."

A friendly smile crinkled the corners of the woman's thin mouth. "Six weeks? Why, that makes you two practically residents!" She extended a hand across the counter. "I'm Helen Broussard."

Valerie accepted the woman's warm, firm handshake. "Valerie Vernon."

The bell on the door jangled as Roger swept in. "Got everything we need, Valerie?"

As he stepped up to the counter, Valerie frowned at the pile of goods she'd accumulated on the countertop. "I think so. You didn't exactly give me time to make a list."

Roger shrugged as he drew out his wallet and asked Helen to total up their purchases.

Helen rang up the food and took some money from Roger for the gas and staples. "You two come back, now, if you need anything else," she told them as she handed Roger his change.

"Oh, we'll be heading this way again," Valerie replied. "I'll be mailing film at the post office in Meadville each week."

"Film?" Helen asked.

Valerie nodded toward Roger, who was replacing his wallet in his back pocket. "We're doing a bird book together."

If Helen was startled by this bit of information, like a typical country person, she didn't let on. "Oh, yes. Lots of pretty birds around these parts—especially this time of year."

As Valerie moved to pick up one of the two bags of groceries, Roger stepped forward and said, "I can handle both of these."

Helen winked at Valerie and said, "My, honey, you sure do have a nice husband. Real cute, too."

Valerie felt herself blushing. When she glanced awkwardly at Roger, she found his eyes were gleaming with some private devilment. "He's not my husband," she said as evenly as possible.

Helen took this bit of information in stride, too, laughing and telling the couple once again that she'd hope to see them soon. But as for Roger, Valerie could have sworn she spotted a silly grin on his face as they swept out the door.

WHEN THEY ARRIVED at the recreation area in Homochitto National Forest, Valerie stretched her legs and looked out at the lovely, rippling lake while Roger spoke with the ranger and got directions to their cabin.

Moments later they were snaking down a narrow dirt road, heading far away from the camping and picnic areas. Valerie glanced about in perplexity, noting that the road kept getting increasingly narrow, the trees and vegetation on either side much denser. As they climbed a narrow, steep rise, she held her breath, then sighed as they started downhill.

"Roger, this is dangerous," she told him with a frown. "What if we should meet another car?"

He laughed. "We're not too likely to meet anyone else on this road. The cabin we'll be staying in has scarcely been used in years."

She frowned. "You mentioned that it's a deserted forestry station?"

He nodded. "Years ago, rangers scouted for forest fires from lookout towers—thus the need for the cabin nearby. But now, planes routinely scan the trees for signs of smoke."

"I see. And just how did you rate use of the cabin?"

He smiled. "One of our New York congressmen is an old family friend. He pulled a few strings in the Department of the Interior for me."

"I'm impressed."

"Well, it would have been practically pointless for us to come here and stay in the public areas. All the campers and hikers would have made bird-watching difficult and frustrating. Besides," Roger continued drolly, "I prefer having you all to myself, deep in the woods where no one can hear your screams."

She laughed. "Surely you jest!"

He chuckled. "Well, I must admit that it did my ego good to hear that shopkeeper assume you were my wife."

"It did?" Valerie's heart increased its tempo.

He nodded, still chuckling. "Considering the difference in our ages, most people wouldn't jump to such a conclusion."

Valerie rolled her eyes. "You're not exactly ancient."

He winked at her. "Well, I'm definitely too old to take on a wife who's still a little wet behind the ears."

Valerie glowered at him, not at all amused by what he obviously felt was a clever rejoinder. She especially resented his implication that she'd even *want* to marry him, should he deign to ask her. "Well, you could always marry me then hire a baby-sitter," she told him sweetly.

That seemed to give him pause. "I meant no offense. I just found it rather amusing that—"

"I think you've said quite enough," she cut in.

He shrugged and returned his attention to his driving, while she suffered her indignation in private. Roger was telling her in his inimitable way that, while he enjoyed having his ego stroked like any male animal, he still wasn't taking seriously the idea of having a romance with someone like her.

So why was this news? she asked herself. Hadn't he made it clear from the start that he considered her to be little more than a child? And from the very moment she'd met him, hadn't his blatant message been that while she turned him on sexually, she just wasn't his type?

Moments later Roger wheeled the car around a curve into a clearing, and Valerie glanced ahead at a small, rustic A-frame cabin.

"Oh, it's precious!" she exclaimed to Roger, glancing approvingly at the cedar cottage, which stood on sturdy posts with a wide railed porch in front. Noting the accumulation of pine needles on the shingled roof, as well as on the porch, she added, "But it does look as if no one has stayed here in years, and—" she cleared her throat "—isn't it rather tiny?"

"Small . . . but adequate," he concurred, braking the car to a stop. He hopped out and came around to her door. "Come on. Let's have a look around."

They climbed the steps to the porch, and Roger kicked pine needles out of the way, then turned over the mat. "Aha! Here's the key, right where the ranger said it would be." Straightening, he unlocked the door and pushed it open with a labored creak.

Inside, a close mustiness greeted them, a disappointment after the invigorating pine-scented air outside. Roger flipped on the light. "Electricity—just as promised!"

She looked around, noting that the inside of the cabin was quite cozy. Almost half of the interior was taken up by a long, narrow living area with a flagstone fireplace along one wall at the center of the cabin. Beyond the fireplace, on the right stretched a small open kitchen, while an open door to the left revealed a glimpse of bunk beds in a tiny bedroom. Close to the bedroom door, a sturdy ladder led to a loft.

The cabin's greatest charm was a high, sawn timber ceiling that gave the small structure a sense of openness it otherwise would have lacked. The freestanding brick chimney stretching up through the roof added another rustic touch, while a wide window in the ceiling above the loft afforded a cobweb-framed view of the sky.

Walking about the living area, Valerie noted with dismay the layers of dust that were everywhere—all over the vinyl sofa and matching chair, the pine dining table and chairs near the kitchen. The dark drapes on the front window looked as if they needed a good shaking, too.

"Well, Valerie?" Roger asked her.

She turned to smile at him. "It's nice—if a bit dusty."

"It'll clean up just great," he assured her, rubbing his hands together as he headed for the kitchen.

She followed, watching him take a tin of matches from a shelf and light the small white enamel stove. He glanced approvingly at the bluish flame. "The ranger said the man was supposed to have filled the propane tank yesterday, so we'll have a stove and heat for the mornings, if we should need it."

Valerie nodded, going off to explore a storeroom behind the kitchen. She nodded her satisfaction. The shelves lining the room would hold most of their food and equipment. She went back through the kitchen, passing Roger, who was now tinkering with the refrigerator. She proceeded on into the bedroom. There was no dresser, though the small closet would suffice for her things. She tested the plastic-covered mattress on the bottom bunk and found it adequate.

Hearing a sound behind her, Valerie turned to find Roger standing in the doorway. His eyes were sweeping over her, and all at once, she was very conscious of their isolation here—and especially of the overpowering male aura Roger exuded in this small room.

"Umm—there's only one bedroom," she told him.

He stepped inside, smiling. "I've noticed." Winking at her, he added, "Top bunk or bottom?"

"Roger!"

He chuckled. "Don't worry, I'm planning to sleep in the loft."

"I see." She glanced around awkwardly. "You could take one of the mattresses."

"That's okay. I brought my own along."

He went back into the living room, and she followed him. "Roger?"

"Yes?"

"Where's the bathroom?"

He grinned. "Look out the kitchen window."

"You're kidding!"

"Nope. And be thankful it's there, and in one piece. Once, while I was staying at an isolated cabin in the Canadian wilderness, the door blew off the damn contraption, and it was twenty below outside."

She giggled. "Well, I suppose things could be worse." Clearing her throat, she added, "I take it there's no shower, either?"

"No. But the ranger told me we're welcome to use the park bathhouse at any time. We'll probably drive down there once a day."

She nodded, then helped Roger unload the car. While he set up a hummingbird feeder on the porch, she went to the bedroom and made up her bunk. Since the day had grown a lot warmer and the cabin was closed and musty, she decided to change into old cutoffs and a T-shirt before helping Roger tackle the massive cleanup the cabin would need.

Her first task was a vigorous sweeping of the wooden floor in the living room. She could hear Roger humming as he worked in the kitchen behind her, and the sound of his deep voice was oddly comforting.

As she swept near the front door, a sudden, fluttering motion outside the window caught her attention. Looking up, she saw a tiny hummingbird buzz up to the red feeder Roger had just hung. Valerie tiptoed to the window and watched, captivated, as the small bird sucked nectar from a flower-shaped feeding stem at the base of the device.

"How precious," she breathed, noting the bird's needle-like beak, its white breast and dark green back. But the bird's wings enchanted her the most. They vibrated so fast that they veiled the miniature bird in a halo of perpetual motion. The movements were utterly poetic as the bird alternately sucked at then retreated from the feeder.

Valerie was in for an even more dazzling spectacle as another hummingbird flew up, this one with a brilliant red throat. Suddenly the two birds were everywhere—over, under and around the feeder, busily flitting at the food and each other. By turns, they chased each other, titillating, then withdrawing, feeding on the nectar and each other. Valerie felt her heart warming as she realized the eventual conclusion of the romantic little vignette. The two birds belonged together. It was so right.

"They're mating," she heard a deep voice pronounce.

Valerie whirled, her face hot. Roger was standing about ten feet away from her. His expression was oddly intense as he looked her over thoroughly.

Despite his heated stare, she braved a smile. "They're beautiful, Roger," she told him. "What kind of—I mean, species of—"

"They're ruby-throated hummingbirds," he told her, taking a step closer, still staring at her in her skimpy clothing. "It's springtime, you know—the mating season, breeding plumage and all that." Again he eyed her meaningfully, then coughed and added, "Aren't you cold in that garb, Valerie?"

"Not at all," she answered. "It's musty in here, and actually, I'm quite comfortable."

"You should be wearing shoes," he said, looking down at her bare feet.

"Maybe I just like going natural."

"Like the birds?" he supplied cynically. "In springtime?"

She glowered at him. Before she could reply, he pointed at her feet and added, "Don't say I didn't warn you about the shoes."

Watching him turn and stride back toward the kitchen, she gritted her teeth. She knew he was right about her feet—the floor was quite splintery—but she'd be damned if she'd admit it. Why had Roger become so angry and disapproving just because she'd put on a T-shirt and cutoffs? He'd seemed so human in the car this morning.

But then she remembered bits and pieces of their conversation—his society background, his family's connections with the congressman from New York. Maybe he was just a rich snob, and seeing her dressed this way reminded him of what a small-town hick she was. And hadn't he found the idea of being married to someone like her laughable? Indeed, he'd chuckled all the way out here from Helen's store.

Valerie was so lost in these unsettling thoughts that she didn't watch where she was going. A few minutes later, Roger found her sitting on the couch trying to pluck a splinter from her foot.

"I told you so," he said self-righteously.

She glowered up at him. "Do you mind? I'm trying to get this splinter out of—"

"And you haven't even cleaned off the skin." Scolding her with his index finger, he added, "Leave that alone until I come back."

She sighed her exasperation, but knew better than to cross him. He went to the kitchen, returning shortly with a first-aid kit. He sat down on the coffee table across from the couch and placed Valerie's foot in his lap. He carefully cleaned the ball of her foot with cotton dipped in alcohol, then plucked out the splinter with tweezers.

"There," he said. But he didn't release her foot. Instead he stroked the arch with his fingertips and stared down at her leg.

"Thank you," she said awkwardly.

He looked up, his gaze meeting hers. His eyes were gleaming with a feral light, and when he spoke, his voice was thick. "You're welcome." His fingertips slid up to her ankle, and his gaze darkened. "No more bare feet. Okay?"

She struggled not to shudder at his provocative touch, smiling at him crookedly and saying, "Right, doctor."

Now the errant fingers were stroking her calf. "Valerie—"

"Yes?" she asked breathlessly.

He swallowed hard. "Do you have any idea how soft you are?"

For a moment they stared at each other, the silence charged. Valerie was certain that at any moment Roger was going to kiss her.

Then he surprised her by cursing under his breath and releasing her foot. He stood, then stunned her by hauling her up into his arms.

"Roger!" she exclaimed as he carried her toward the bedroom.

"You don't think I'm going to let you walk around on that foot until you put on clean socks, do you?" he asked testily. "All I need is you with blood poisoning or something."

"Well, you don't have to get so angry about it. Believe me, I'll try my best not to inconvenience you by dying!"

But he didn't seem to have heard her as he continued toward the bedroom, rolling his eyes as he mumbled under his breath, "Why did I come out here with a veritable child, anyway? A mature woman would never wear something so provocative."

"Roger!"

By now he was inside the bedroom, summarily dumping her on the bottom bunk. Without even asking her permission, he began rummaging through her open suitcase on the upper bunk. Pulling out a pair of scarlet lace panties, he blinked at them rapidly. Then he tossed the wisp down, as if the flaming fabric had just scorched his hand. A moment later he tossed Valerie a pair of clean socks.

Valerie was appalled, horrified to think that Roger might have found her diaphragm in a zippered compartment of her suitcase. "Good grief, what did I do to you?" she demanded angrily.

He stared down at her, breathing hard. "I don't think you want me to answer that question right now. But I will say this—wear those cutoffs again and you won't be wearing them for long."

"Crudely put," she snapped at him.

"But accurately," he snapped back. He picked up her hiking boots from the floor beneath the bunk and handed them to her with exaggerated courtesy. "Don't forget shoes," he said as he turned and strode out of the room.

Furious, Valerie threw a boot after him, but it only hit the door after he closed it.

OUTSIDE VALERIE'S ROOM, Roger shook his head and groaned, wincing as he felt Valerie's boot thudding against the closed door. It had been so long since he'd been with a truly young woman and had seen all the sexy, skimpy things they wore—and didn't wear!

He'd thought being with Valerie on Sunday had been torture, when he'd watched her with Rico and had observed how well the two contemporaries had gotten along. Yet being alone with her here was a thousand times worse. When he'd touched her just now, when he'd looked at her lovely bare legs and into her vibrant blue-violet eyes—all he could think of was hauling her into his arms again, having that gorgeous, slim body wrapped around him.

And here in the woods, there was no Rico waiting in the wings to stop him or give him second thoughts.

Didn't the woman have any idea what she was doing to him? How on earth would he endure six weeks of this type of exquisite frustration?

He'd never make it.

6

VALERIE AND ROGER were stiffly formal with each other during lunch. He had surprised her by preparing the meal himself.

Valerie had wisely changed back into her jeans and a white long-sleeved shirt and had also donned her socks and hiking boots, just as Roger had ordered. She remained flabbergasted and resentful regarding his angry reaction to seeing her in her cutoffs, his taunts about her immaturity and foolishness. Why blame her because he found her casual clothing sexually provocative? Why not pull his own mind out of the gutter?

Roger was behaving as if the entire incident had never occurred. All through lunch, he'd been delivering a scholarly lecture on ornithology, ostensibly to initiate Valerie into the world of warblers. Aside from his interest in her as a protégé he was training, he didn't seem to know she existed.

"Most people don't realize that many birds live, breed and feed within inches of the ground," he was now informing her. "But you'll find out this afternoon."

She set down her fork and looked up. "This afternoon?"

"Yes. We're going on a hike so that I may acquaint you with the basics of spotting and photographing warblers."

"I see."

"I won't be available to coach you the entire time we're here," he warned her, "since I've much writing to complete. So let's hope you're a quick study."

"I will be," Valerie replied, unable to keep a note of defensiveness from creeping into her voice.

Roger didn't comment as he got up and moved toward the kitchen. She watched him take a pan of beans and franks from the small stove. Irresistibly her eyes swept over him. He looked good in his jeans, she reflected with a sudden sinking feeling. They fit him snugly, hugging every masculine contour. He'd rolled up the sleeves of his flannel shirt in order to cook, and his bare forearms were tanned and hard muscled. Perhaps she should make a comment about *him* wearing something provocative!

No, that would only convince him that her thoughts and motives were wandering in the wrong direction—which they doubtless were. She should know better!

He moved back toward her now, the sun dancing in his gray-streaked hair and brown eyes. Holding the pan out toward her, he asked, "More beans and franks?"

She shook her head, trying not to focus on his hand holding the pan, trying not to remember the way he had touched her, carried her to the bedroom, half an hour earlier.

"Suit yourself," he was saying as he sat down and scooped more of the food onto his plate. "But as for me, I'm famished. It's truly invigorating how the great outdoors gives one such an appetite."

"Ah, yes, the great outdoors," she murmured ironically. She set down her napkin. "Well, while you finish eating, I think I'll just tidy up the kitchen. We don't want to be late for my instructional hike to meet our fine feathered friends, now do we?"

He didn't answer as she stood, took her plate and moved back to the kitchen. But she caught him staring at her for a moment, his expression guarded. Then he returned his attention to the food.

At the sink, Valerie frowned as she ran a panful of soapy water. So the great outdoors gave Roger Benedict an appetite, she thought to herself. It was obvious that carrying a provocatively clad female to the bedroom came in a distant second.

WHEN VALERIE JOINED ROGER in the living room fifteen minutes later, she was shocked to see what looked like four sections of green plastic piping laid out on the floor next to the couch.

"Snake leggings," he replied to her puzzled look as he got to his feet. "The extra pair was to have been for Rico. But one size fits all, so they're yours."

"Snake leggings?" she repeated, feeling a small twinge in her stomach. It occurred to her that she had not really considered the full implication of photographing birds in a wilderness area. While she had been a Girl Scout, she was hardly the seasoned outdoorsman Roger was. Yet she tried not to show her misgivings as she pointed at the plastic devices and said brightly, "They look like lopped-off pieces of medieval armor, complete with the green decay of centuries."

Roger laughed. "An apt description. Actually, the green color is for camouflage. We don't want to scare off our fine feathered friends, as you call them." He nodded toward her. "Now come here. I'll show you how to work them."

Valerie moved forward, and Roger knelt by her feet. Following his instructions, she stepped into the expandable contraptions. The tops flared to accomodate the shape of her calves, and the open bottoms rested on the tops of her hiking boots.

She cleared her throat. "Are you expecting many snakes out there?"

His lips twitched as he got to his feet. "Most snakes are harmless, and even the harmful varieties want to stay out of your path, if possible. But since we'll be hiking through heavy brush, better safe than sorry, right? You might step on a copperhead or something."

Valerie's skin crawled. "Step on a copperhead?"

His eyes narrowed. "There's no place for a squeamish woman out here, so if you're having second thoughts—"

"Heavens, no!" she said with bravado, waving him off. "Throw on your snake leggings and let's get cracking."

Chuckling, he did as she bid. Moments later, as they prepared to leave, Roger suddenly took her arm, restraining her. "Look, the hummingbirds are back," he said, pointing toward the front window.

Valerie turned to observe the hummingbirds at the feeder. They were so sweet, romantically flitting about, flirting with each other and sucking at the nectar.

Spring mating rituals, she thought, remembering Roger's earlier words.

"The one with the ruby throat is the male," he was telling her in a low voice as he observed the tiny creatures with avid interest. "The female of the species wears the usual dull colors, as one might expect."

She shot him a withering look. "Spoken like a true chauvinist."

He chuckled. "No, it's true. The female always wears the less vibrant colors." Pausing to eye her up and down, he caught a long breath. "However, I'd have to make an exception in your case. That auburn hair, those bright eyes. You're nothing if not colorful."

She shot him a perturbed look as he moved closer. "So your convenient formula doesn't always fit, does it, Roger?"

"No, it doesn't." All at once, Roger Benedict actually looked contrite as he edged even closer to her. "About what I said—did—earlier . . ."

Then abruptly their snake leggings clinked and the spell was broken.

"Well," Valerie said with forced cheerfulness, stepping away from him. "Perhaps we'd best get to work before our trusty armor turns rusty."

A NARROW PATH LED from the cabin into the woods. Valerie followed Roger, his extra pair of binoculars hanging from her neck, and her camera, complete with telephoto lens, suspended from her shoulder strap. The stiff plastic snake leggings felt awkward against her calves as she hiked along, though Roger, a few feet ahead of her, seemed comfortable as he strode down the trail carrying his binoculars and a cassette recorder.

As they crossed a plank bridge over a clear, flowing stream, Valerie smiled, watching sunshine sift through the ceiling of trees above them, showering the water with an exquisite light play. She had always appreciated the beauty of the outdoors and now drew deep breaths of pine-scented air into her lungs. Here, in these peaceful surroundings, she felt almost as if the hustle and bustle of civilization did not exist. It had been a long time since she'd been in an isolated setting like this, and she could well understand Roger's love for nature.

Shortly after they passed the bridge, the trail abruptly ended on the crest of a small rise where a forestry tower stood. "It's deserted now, like the cabin," Roger explained as they both stared at the weathered structure. "We'll probably hear planes passing over at times, to scout the trees for fires." He glanced upward. "I'm planning to climb the tower occasionally to scan for birds in the treetops."

From this point, they proceeded directly into the woods. The small trail served only to connect the cabin with the lookout tower. As they navigated through the underbrush and trees, Valerie was grateful for the snake leggings, since it was often difficult to see what was at her feet in the shadowy forest. However, surprisingly once they got a few yards beyond the brush lining the trail, the landscape cleared somewhat, and they entered a forest carpeted with pine needles and sprinkled with clumps of ferns and iridescent-looking shrubs.

"It's breathtaking," Valerie whispered, looking awestruck at a huge glossy magnolia tree and inhaling the sweet perfume of its large white blossoms.

Roger nodded, turning back to her. "Just stop and listen a moment."

Valerie listened carefully to the primitive sounds surrounding her—the rustle of pine needles in the wind, the chirping of birds, the flowing of the stream several hundred yards behind them.

Then abruptly Valerie slapped her neck and glanced perplexed at her hand. "Mosquitoes—in April?"

Roger chuckled as he took her hand and brushed the squashed mosquito from her palm. "Oh, yes. They are a bird-watcher's plague."

"But I didn't get any bites when I walked around the campground this morning."

"We're now far away from areas that might be fogged. No matter, though—next time, we'll douse you with repellent. Our best bet for now is to keep moving."

As they continued on, she slapped another mosquito on her wrist. "Why don't they go after you?" she asked Roger resentfully.

He laughed and called over his shoulder, "Oh, I suppose I'm too old and crusty for them. Mosquitoes have a sweet tooth, I presume. They like young, sweet things like you."

Valerie groaned and waved him on while her other hand slapped a mosquito trying to bite her thigh through the thick denim of her jeans. What intrepid little beasts these insects were!

Soon they arrived at a large clearing. Roger motioned for Valerie to sit on a tree stump in the sun, just inside the circle of trees. Then he moved to the center of the grassy opening, placing his cassette recorder on the ground and punching on a tape.

When he returned to her side, she glanced at him in confusion as a shrill sound emanated from the recorder.

He smiled and seated himself next to her on the large
stump. "It's a recording of a screech owl. All birds hate
screech owls, because the owl attacks other birds at night.
Therefore, when a screech owl enters an area, all the other
birds will band together to mob him and chase him off. So
get your camera ready, Valerie. You should be able to get
some good shots shortly."

"How interesting," she murmured back, removing the lens
cover on her camera and keeping her gaze riveted on the recorder. Listening to the high-pitched, almost humorous
screeching, she gave Roger an amazed smile. She was certainly learning some fascinating things about birds today.
And it was nice sitting here with him in the clearing; the sun
was beating down pleasantly on her back, and for the moment the mosquitoes weren't biting.

Adjusting the telephoto lens on her camera, Valerie asked
him in a whisper, "Do you photograph many birds yourself?"

He shrugged. "I'm a fairly skilled amateur. I have to be because I don't always have a professional photographer along
when I bird-watch. But for the book, the photographs must
be top-notch."

"They will be," she put in rather defensively.

He smiled. "Right. That's why I have you along."

"Right."

They waited in patient silence for a few more minutes, and
just as Roger had predicted, the first bird flew in—a bright
red cardinal. He landed close to the recorder and began
pecking at the ground nearby. Almost simultaneously a
scolding sound came from a bush a few feet away. "It's a
Carolina wren," Roger explained in a hushed voice, pointing out a buff-and-brown colored bird flitting about in the
underbrush.

Valerie watched with interest as more birds flew in—red birds, blue birds, brown birds, multicolored birds—some with long beaks, some with long tail feathers, some with top notches. Soon the ground and the surrounding bushes were teeming with birds—chirping, angry birds of every size and color, some of them pecking at the ground or even at the recorder itself, some egging the others on from the sidelines. All were searching for the offensive screech owl and were quite chagrined that they could not find him.

Looking at the vast choir of birds, Valerie shook her head. "Well, I'll be damned," she muttered to Roger. "It really does work."

Roger identified each species to Valerie. Some had exotic, descriptive names, such as white-eyed vireo, brown thrasher and wood thrush. Other names ranged from the amusing to the absurd, such as yellow-bellied sapsucker, blue-gray gnatcatcher and tufted titmouse.

A few minutes later, Roger pointed toward the brush at the edge of the clearing. "Look, the warblers are starting to come in."

At once she slid to her knees at the side of the stump, lifting her camera and squinting in the direction of Roger's hand. "What? Where?" she whispered to him tensely.

She heard him slide to his knees behind her. "Watch closely. Put your camera down for now and just use your binoculars. Warblers are small and difficult to spot."

Valerie followed Roger's instructions, soon deciding that his last remark was the understatement of the year. She stared as intently as she could through the binoculars, but saw nothing except an occasional flutter of motion.

"Here, let me help you," she heard Roger say gruffly.

As Valerie continued to scan the brush, she felt Roger positioning himself closer behind her, placing a knee between her spread calves and pressing his chest against her back. She felt a tingle of sexual excitement at his nearness, but was soon distracted by his rather terse instructions.

"Put down your binoculars—" his hand pulled the binoculars away from her face "—and just look at the brush until you spot some motion. There, look straight ahead, about a foot above the ground."

She stared at the place he had indicated and at last spotted a flurry of wings. She heard Roger say, "Okay, you've spotted him now. Slowly raise your binoculars. But remember—don't move your eyes."

She followed Roger's instructions carefully, and a few seconds later, she zeroed in on the warbler. It was a tiny, precious creature with a white belly, black-and-white striped back and yellow on its crown, wings and rump.

"It's a myrtle warbler," she heard Roger say.

"Why, it's hardly bigger than a hummingbird!" she gasped excitedly. She lowered her binoculars and raised her camera. But the warbler was already gone. "Oh, damn!" she muttered.

"Patience, dear," she heard Roger say.

During the next few minutes, Roger helped her spot several more species of warblers. But, true to his earlier predictions, they were all extremely small, nervous and jumpy creatures. She'd no sooner raise her camera than they'd be gone. Now she knew exactly what Rico Romero had meant when he had called spotting and photographing warblers "exquisite frustration."

Then at last, she knew a nominal amount of success, as she captured an orange crown warbler with her camera. "Got him!" she cried exultantly to Roger, shifting to smile up at him. But she moved too suddenly and practically knocked them both off balance. Roger's arms clenched about her waist as he struggled to steady them both on their knees. By the time he got them stabilized, her face was mere inches from his, her bottom wedged snugly against the hard front of his trousers. A hot current of excitement shot through her as his smoldering eyes bored down into hers. She felt so dizzy and breathless she was glad he held her tightly.

For a long, charged moment, they continued to stare at each other, her cheeks growing warmer, his breath quick and hot on her face. Then he said irritably, "Watch it, Valerie. I don't exactly have in mind a tumble in the underbrush this afternoon."

She shot him a resentful glance as he abruptly released her and stood. The screech owl tape had stopped, and the birds were flying off. Declining his offer of a helping hand, she got to her feet, brushing off her knees. "Are you going to reset the tape?" she asked him stiffly.

He shook his head. "The birds know we're here now. But we'll remember this location and come back later." Flicking dirt off his jeans, he added, "Let's head back."

Sighing, Valerie followed Roger out of the clearing. She had enjoyed having him near her earlier—enjoyed it far too much!

But why was it every time they got the least bit close physically, Roger got mad at her?

It was going to be a very long six weeks, she realized grimly.

ROGER WAS SILENT as they hiked back toward the cabin. Following him, Valerie thought of their fascinating experience in the clearing. She had to admire Roger—he certainly knew what he was doing. It must have taken him years to learn to spot those tiny warblers. This last thought brought a rush of uneasiness as she realized all she would have to learn and accomplish in a mere six weeks. Would she ever be able to spot and photograph these elusive little creatures on her own?

Even more unsettling was the remembrance of having Roger kneel behind her—the feeling of being nestled against his solid strength—even if just to bird-watch. Her stomach lurched slightly as she recalled staring up at him, their mouths mere inches apart.

Yet why had he gotten so angry and defensive about it all?

"Freeze, Valerie!"

Roger's terse whisper wrenched Valerie from her thoughts and made her stop violently in her tracks. She glanced downward anxiously, certain that there must be a snake somewhere in their path. As a child, she'd had a bad experience with a snake, and she wasn't looking to repeat it. But she spotted nothing on the trail. Instead she watched Roger slowly raise his binoculars and gaze off steadily to the east. Obviously he had spotted another bird.

"Is it another warbler?" she whispered, hoping to get more photographs.

"No, just hush," came his mumbled reply.

Frowning, Valerie tried to remain still and wait patiently. But they were deep in the shadows of the woods again, and the mosquitoes were once again attacking. This time, since she wasn't moving, they descended in force, biting even her mouth and ears. For excruciating moments, she tried to be still, yet inevitably the torture grew too intense, and she began slapping vigorously at the bugs.

At once there was a fluttering noise in a nearby tree; then Roger turned on her angrily. "Damn it, Valerie! There was a winter wren in that tree, a very rare species. And now you've scared it off!"

"But, Roger, I—"

Yet before she could explain, he swung about and headed off again. Gritting her teeth, she followed him.

To Valerie's deepening chagrin, this maddening ritual was repeated again and again as Roger stopped to spot additional birds. Each time, Roger expected her to remain still as a statue, and each time, the mosquitoes descended on her in force. But Valerie gritted her teeth and tried her best to weather the attacks in stoic silence. She'd be damned if she was going to complain again, thus proving to Roger that she was a "typical woman" and couldn't hack it!

Then, just when Valerie's patience was nearing the breaking point, Roger stopped to watch a red-shouldered hawk sitting in a tree. He seemed captivated, even spellbound, as he gazed up through his binoculars, watching the large brown-and-red bird scan for prey from its perch on a high branch. Several feet away from him, Valerie leaned against a magnolia tree, brushing off mosquitoes as unobtrusively as possible and tapping her foot in betrayal of her mounting exasperation.

When her watch attested that they had stood in this same spot for over twenty minutes, something snapped inside her, and she found herself informing Roger, with scarcely veiled sarcasm, "I don't know how to tell you this, but he's much too big to be a warbler."

Feathers flapped at Valerie's words, and the hawk flew off, screeching "Eek, eek, eek!" as if offended by her remark.

Roger turned angrily on Valerie, then a stunned expression replaced his ire. "My God, Valerie! You're covered with mosquito bites. Why didn't you say something?"

For a moment she glared at him, then her eyes crossed as another mosquito landed on the tip of her nose. "Mosquitoes? What mosquitoes?" she quipped.

Roger hurried to her side, whisking the pest from her nose. "Come on, let's get you back and put some ointment on those bites." Sheepishly he added, "Sorry, Valerie. At times, I tend to be a bit self-absorbed."

"A bit?" she repeated incredulously, brushing past him and continuing on toward the cabin.

Within ten minutes, they had left the brush and emerged near the lookout tower. But as they crossed the bridge over the stream, Roger suddenly paused, the binoculars flashing quickly to his eyes.

"Valerie!" he whispered in a voice thick with excitement. "Come here, quick, and get this shot for me. Just downstream, there's a green heron about to spear a fish."

Valerie stopped in her tracks, staring at Roger in amazement. This man was unbelievable! Now that he was aware of her discomfort, how could he be so insensitive as to ask her to stop again? She was covered with welts, yet he expected her to—

"Valerie!" His hoarse voice cut into her thoughts. "Hurry, or you'll miss the shot."

The devil with the shot! Valerie swore to herself silently. Clenching her jaw, she set down her camera and binoculars, both of which had grown ten times heavier during their journey. Slowly she approached Roger's broad back.

He was still watching the bird intently and did not notice her advancing toward him on the bridge. For a delicious moment she thought of pushing him into the stream. But the more cautious side of her nature overrode her vindictiveness, so she simply opted to make a face at him behind his back. It was childish, perhaps, but felt wonderful under the circumstances!

Unfortunately, that's when Roger turned, jabbing Valerie in the midriff with his elbow and knocking her into the stream.

At first she was too stunned to react, as the shock of cold water hit her and a hard rock jabbed her bottom. Then instinctively she tried to struggle to her feet, only to slip on the mossy rocks and fall once more on her behind, cold water splashing all over her face and hair and into her eyes.

Flabbergasted, she simply sat in the stream for a moment, in water up to her waist, trying to gather her wits as she swept globs of sopping wet hair from her face and eyes.

It was then that she heard Roger laughing. She looked up to see him standing above her on the bridge, laughing so hard she expected he might topple in at any moment, too.

"You should see yourself!" he cried, his wanton mirth bringing tears to his eyes.

With as much dignity as she could muster, Valerie struggled to her feet. She almost lost her balance again, then steadied herself. Her hiking boots were filled with water, as were her snake leggings, and remaining stable took a monumental effort. She shot Roger a withering glance and extended her hand. "Help me out!"

He eyed her suspiciously. "Valerie, you wouldn't—er—"

"Help me out, damn it!"

He stepped forward, grinning sheepishly, and extended his hand. She took his hand, but unfortunately, that's when she struggled for her footing again and pulled Roger in with her.

Water spewed in every direction as both of them landed on the rocky creek bottom. Seconds later they were both sitting in the stream, glaring at each other. Roger's glasses were covered with water, but Valerie could readily tell that the look in his eyes was absolutely scathing.

"Sorry," she said lamely.

He didn't reply, but abruptly whipped off his glasses. She noted that his eyes were burning with an entirely different emotion as he stared pointedly at the swell of her bosom. A muscle twitched in his strong jaw. Looking downward, Valerie was horrified to see the lacy imprint of her bra, as well as the taut outline of her nipples, all brazenly visible through the drenched white fabric of her shirt.

Almost violently she crossed her arms over her breasts. "Are you all right?" she asked Roger awkwardly, her face feeling scalded despite the coldness of the water.

His only reply was a feral grunt as he shoved his glasses into his pocket, struggled to his feet and stamped out of the stream. As he climbed the bank and returned to the bridge, Valerie reflected that Roger Benedict was the only person she'd ever known who could pull off being dunked in a stream fully clothed and still maintain his dignity. However, his wet clothing also hugged every inch of his male strength, and a very obvious bulge at the front of his trousers bespoke his inner agitation. She marveled at his aroused state, recalling that cold water was usually supposed to dampen a man's ardor. Thinking of how ludicrous the entire situation was, she almost giggled. But then, glimpsing Roger's murderous expression, she thought better of the impulse.

He pulled out his glasses, shaking them slightly to get rid of the moisture as he glowered down at her. He spoke with consummate sarcasm. "If you don't mind, Valerie, I don't think I'll try to help you out again. I might not survive a second attempt."

With this, he whipped on his glasses, squared his shoulders and strode off.

Valerie sighed as she once again struggled to her feet, then climbed out of the stream, gathering her equipment. Roger had just accused her of pulling him in on purpose, and in truth, she didn't want to examine her own motives too closely there, because she was afraid of what she might find.

But, damn it, the man had maddened her. Rico had warned her that Roger was a fanatic about birds, but she'd thought he was only joking. Now she knew much better. Now she knew that when Roger had gotten angry at her in the clearing, the heat hadn't come just from their nearness. No, he'd doubtless heartily resented the fact that her inexperience was slowing him down in achieving his goals for his book. Ditto, their dip in the stream.

And, given his physical response just now, he was obviously still mad at her for being "provocative," for wantonly distracting him from his more pressing purpose.

One thing was certain, she thought dismally as she plodded off. Roger Benedict cared a lot more about the birds than he did about the birds and the bees.

7

"I'M GOING, NOW."

It was the next morning. Valerie stood at the edge of the kitchen, wearing jeans and a long-sleeved shirt, and heavily laden with her photography and bird-watching regalia.

Roger sat across from her at the dining table. He did not look up at her words, but stared moodily at some notes laid out in front of him.

Roger had been cool and distant toward her ever since their little dip in the stream yesterday. Last night he'd buried his head in a book on ornithology while playing nonstop recordings of birdcalls. Valerie had wisely resisted complaining, even though the loud, ludicrous-sounding calls had still been trilling out when she went to bed.

She edged closer to him, clearing her throat nervously. "I just thought I'd tell you that I'm going now."

"I heard you the first time." His voice was clipped, and again he did not look up.

Valerie inched even closer, thoroughly perplexed now as she studied him and the work he had laid out on the table. He wore a short-sleeved plaid shirt, its open neck revealing a hint of the dark curly hair on his chest. His legs, clad in the familiar jeans, were extended out comfortably beneath the table, his feet in brown oxfords. But despite his casual dress, he looked erudite and intimidating as he sifted through stacks of notes lettered with neat penmanship, then picked up one of the many books in a stack nearby.

Valerie's heart fluttered. Roger looked so intense and handsome sitting there, his mouth all the more sexy because he was scowling. He was a maddening devil, all right; yet guilt over yesterday's dunking incident spurred her to try to smooth things over between them.

"Those are your notes, I take it?" she asked.

"Brilliant, Valerie." Still, he did not look up at her.

Damn, he was unreachable! she thought to herself. Nevertheless, she continued, "They're not typed."

This time, he did look up, whipping off his glasses. "No, my notes are not typed. That's why I have a secretary back in New York."

"I just think it's rather odd that you're a writer and you don't type," she continued defensively. "In the movies, writers are always pecking away at a typewriter."

He stared at her, tapping his fingers restlessly.

She inched even closer. "Hmmm... I see you have impeccable penmanship."

"So what if I do?"

She tilted her chin. "Don't tell me you're one of those neurotic perfectionist types? I bet that back in New York, all your suits are hanging precisely one inch apart in your closet."

"Will you kindly get the hell out of here?" he asked.

She sighed her frustration, still not willing to give up. "Well, I suppose you writers must have your eccentricities."

At last a ghost of a smile pulled at his formidable mouth as he eyed her up and down. "We do."

She rested her palms on the tabletop and leaned toward him. "About yesterday—"

He snapped a book shut beneath her nose. "I prefer not to discuss yesterday."

"Just because you—er—accidentally fell in the stream—"

He shot to his feet. "Correction. You pulled me in on purpose."

"Well, even if I did, can you blame me after you laughed at me that way?"

"Yes," he replied baldly.

She gestured her exasperation. "Why are you so mad at me?"

He rounded the table to confront her and spoke with strained patience. "I'm angry at you because now I'm out my hiking boots due to your childish tantrum."

"I'll buy you new ones!"

"It's hardly the price of a new pair of boots that I'm concerned about. We're already behind schedule, and now we'll have to waste a good part of tomorrow hunting for new boots for us both. I imagine yours will be quite uncomfortable today, since wet leather shrinks. Or have you noticed?"

"I've noticed," she said.

"Time is money to me." He glanced at his notes, then pointedly back at her. "And I think we've wasted quite enough of it this morning, don't you?"

"All right! All right! I can take a hint! I'm going!" Feeling defeated and frustrated, she turned and stormed out the back door.

Watching her leave, Roger started to go after her. Then he groaned and collapsed into his chair, cursing under his breath.

VALERIE TRAMPED DOWN the steamy trail in her tight, damp hiking boots. The morning was mild and cool, and fog clung to the landscape, blurring the rolling terrain before her.

She glanced about in confusion as she moved through the haze. "How am I going to find any birds in this muck?" she asked herself in dismay. Had she bitten off more than she could chew with this assignment?

As far as birds went, she was really out on a limb, since Roger had been little help in planning her excursion. Early this morning—right after he'd informed her that she'd be on her own today while he caught up on his writing—he'd simply handed her a pocket bird guide, along with the cassette deck with the recording of the screech owl.

He'd been such a maddening stranger since yesterday. But she'd resolved that she'd be damned if she was going to ask for his help, effectively admitting to him that she couldn't handle this assignment.

Once again assuring herself that she was made of stronger stuff than that, she trudged ahead. Yet she couldn't escape the undeniable fact nagging at the back of her mind—that despite Roger's exasperating behavior, she was still very attracted to him. Perversely, his distance and surliness only intensified her yearning. She was doubtless a fool, since Roger had already warned her that there wouldn't be a future for them. But she couldn't help what she felt.

Remembering her Girl Scout training, Valerie marked her trail as she went along, using bits of red cloth from a kitchen rag. Finally, when her feet were about to kill her, she found the clearing they had visited the previous day. Overcast and dreary now, it seemed almost a different place. Yet a glance at the tree stump where she and Roger had sat confirmed that it was the same spot.

Valerie positioned the cassette recorder in the center of the area, then returned to sit on the stump, waiting, her camera poised, as the familiar screeching came from the machine. She had doused herself with repellent before she left the cabin, so the mosquitoes were leaving her alone.

The birds began to fly in, searching for the offensive owl. Valerie became very busy, alternately fumbling with her bird book, the binoculars and her camera. But no sooner would she get a fix on one of the tiny birds than it would fly off! Soon she was cursing her frustration.

Finally in desperation she laid down the book and the binoculars, concentrating solely on her camera. To heck with trying to identify the various species of warblers. It was sheer hell merely to spot them, period, they were so damn tiny.

Looking steadily through her telephoto lens and scanning the clearing and trees, she mentally reviewed the meager collection of data she had ascertained about warblers: they were tiny, had long, pointed beaks and medium-length tail feathers, and often wore bright blotches of yellow or patches of orange.

Then she began photographing everything that even remotely resembled a warbler—a yellow bird with orange streaks on its breast, a black-and-orange bird with a white belly, a yellow-breasted bird with a steel-gray back and what looked like black beads about its neck. All were busily flitting from branch to branch, chirping noisily as they searched for the source of their irritation.

The shutter snapped rapidly, and by the time the tape concluded, Valerie had shot the entire roll of thirty-six. She even had time to pause once and change to a more powerful 600 mm telephoto lens, so that she could capture a small orange-breasted bird with a black back as it pecked away at insects in the shadows.

Valerie retrieved the recorder and the birds flew off. If she was lucky, perhaps a dozen of the shots would actually be of warblers. If she was luckier still, perhaps one of them would eventually appear in Roger's book. But, like most professional photographers, she was philosophical about the great number of shots that would never be used. She and Roger would screen the hundreds of color slides she planned to take, choosing only the choicest shots to be developed into prints and sent in with the manuscript.

The sun at last appeared, beaming down on the clearing as Valerie pulled out the sandwich and soda she'd brought along for lunch. Maybe it wouldn't be such a bad day, after all, she thought.

BACK AT THE CABIN, Roger was pacing as he glanced at his watch. It was past one o'clock and Valerie still hadn't returned. He was getting worried. And he blamed himself for everything. He had acted like such a jerk this morning, sending her off on her own. She was still so inexperienced. He should have taken her to town to get new boots, then coached her through another session in the woods. But the truth was, he didn't trust himself alone with her. This beautiful, forthright girl was getting to him in every way, and he'd been trying every trick in the book to distance himself from her.

He groaned as his mind swirled with the tormenting images of their time together yesterday. The clearing, when Valerie's sexy little bottom had pressed so provocatively against the front of his trousers, the urge to sink his hands into her jeans and fill his fingers with her softness. The stream, when her shirt had clung so seductively to her breasts, the urge to pull her close and catch one of those lovely taut nipples in his mouth. He realized that he hadn't even minded falling in with her.

But he just couldn't get past the fact that she was all wrong for him.

That didn't excuse his callous behavior, he reminded himself reproachfully. Glancing at his watch, he decided it was high time he went after her. He wasn't getting any work done anyway.

Besides, she could get lost out there. A bear could eat her.

These distressing thoughts made him quickly grab his hiking gear and rush out the back door.

THAT AFTERNOON, Valerie's major accomplishment was to get lost.

She started out doing everything right, following her marked trail back toward the cabin. But then she became distracted as she spotted the first bird she had seen all day that she was certain was a warbler. She even knew its name—blackburnian—a species that had particularly intrigued her as she studied her bird guide over lunch. She had stared at the drawing for a long moment because the bird was so vibrantly colorful. It had a brilliant orange chest and throat, a gray back and a striking black-banded face.

And there it was, on a branch not twenty feet away from her, its colors even more vivid than the drawing as it sang its little heart out!

"I'm going to get you—precious bird," Valerie whispered, raising her camera.

For a few seconds, the warbler cooperated as Valerie snapped the shutter. Then it flitted off, as if teasing her. Though the bird led Valerie on a long and merry chase, she got some excellent shots, capturing the warbler in flight, eating insects off the bark of a tree and wiping its long black bill on a branch.

Then suddenly the bird seemed to tire of the game and flew off to parts unknown.

And just as suddenly, Valerie realized that she was completely lost!

She stared about in bewilderment. Nothing looked familiar. The landscape was steeper, the trees more closely spaced than before.

"Damn," she muttered under her breath. Wouldn't Roger laugh if he could see her now?

She was, however, grateful that at least Roger was back at the cabin. If she was as badly lost as she suspected she was, he might be her only hope of getting out of this mess during the twentieth century.

She glanced about the alien area, trying to decide upon a course of action. Then it occurred to her to look at the sky. It was after two o'clock now, and the sun should be drifting down slightly to the west. The cabin was south of her—that much she was sure of. So if she turned left using the sun as her guide, she would end up at the cabin—or perhaps miles to the east or west of it, who knew?

It was a slim chance, but her only option at the moment. Even if she missed the cabin, she should eventually arrive at the campground or the highway—or so she fervently hoped!

Valerie began hiking in a southerly direction. Her feet were nearly numb from the constriction of her hiking boots, and the mosquitoes were once again attacking her. She should have brought the repellent along, she realized ruefully, slapping at one of the pesky little beasts. But then she hadn't expected to get lost when she left this morning.

On she trudged, and soon her feet felt so wretched she was tempted to cast off her shoes and the offensive snake-leggings as well. But then she saw a fat black snake slither into a bush a few yards ahead of her—the first snake she had seen so far—and thought better of her rash idea.

At one point she heard the buzz of a plane overhead. She screamed and flailed about trying to signal it, but the small green-and-white aircraft flew straight over her and did not return. "You nut," she chided herself. "They're looking for smoke—not a madwoman."

On she marched, for at least a mile, but still nothing looked familiar. Just as she was ready to kick herself for thinking she could hack it in the wilderness, she suddenly heard the sound of rushing water nearby.

"The stream!" she cried, running in the direction of the gurgling sound.

Yes, it was there, just beyond a wall of reeds. "Oh, please, be the same stream!" she implored.

She moved through the reeds onto the grassy bank. It looked like the same stream, she thought, studying the narrow bayou flowing over moss and smooth rocks. And if it was, she could follow it back to the cabin.

She proceeded south along the grassy bank. Below her, moss and ferns carpeted the creek bed, while above her, entwined tree limbs shaded her path. Watching light showers sparkle on the cool rushing waters, she began to feel somewhat calmer.

Then, just as she rounded a small bend in the bayou, she was attacked by the most vicious horde of mosquitoes she had ever encountered in her life. She watched them swarm from the wet grass in a hungry wave, inundating her body like a coating of black spray paint!

"Good heavens! It must be their rookery!" she cried, slapping at them wildly as she raced down the bank. She ran downstream for about a quarter mile, escaping the onslaught as she moved into a wider, more open area of the bayou, where the water gleamed with the blinding light of the full sun, and wide, warm boulders in the stream and along the bank invited sunbathing.

But the tranquil setting was temporarily lost on Valerie, who stood breathing hard as she gazed ahead toward the sky. For there, perhaps a mile beyond her, was the forestry tower!

She whooped with joy at her discovery. She had found her way back, and stuffy old Roger would never know the difference!

With her immediate problem now solved, she paused to glance about the area where she stood. The stream looked so tempting. It was wider and deeper here, the water clean and glowing. Her feet were killing her, and most of her body was again covered with tormenting welts from the mosquito bites.

What the heck! She'd have a dip before she returned, cool down her welts; then Roger would have no inkling whatever of her ordeal, not when she arrived back at the cabin as fresh as a daisy.

In less than a minute, Valerie had stripped naked and stood with the sun beating on her back as she stuck her toes into the bayou. The water was ice-cold as she waded in, but it felt heavenly against the itchy welts on her skin. She moved out to where the stream was about three feet deep, then swam about luxuriantly, savoring the electric coldness of the water against her nude body.

When she emerged a few minutes later, a large boulder near the water's edge beckoned her, and she couldn't resist lying down on it for a few minutes to warm her shivering body. The heat was so soothing that she soon grew sleepy. She couldn't contain a provocative image of Roger there with her as she dozed off in the sunshine. . . .

AN HOUR LATER, VALERIE felt rested and refreshed as she entered the back door of the cabin. Placing her equipment on the shelves in the storeroom, she congratulated herself on not dozing until after sunset. Her nap had been brief, and she had continued back without mishap.

She found Roger in the dining area, still poring over his notes at the table.

"Have a good day?" he asked without looking up.

"Yes. And you?"

He glanced up, taking off his glasses, and she noted with some alarm that there was an intense, peculiar gleam in his eyes.

"You were gone a long time," he said.

She shrugged. "I had a lot to accomplish."

"I got worried about you so I went looking for you."

Her heart skipped a beat. "You did?"

He stood. "Yes, I did. I climbed the tower."

"The forestry tower?" She heard her voice crack.

"That's the only tower around here, isn't it, sweetheart?"

Roger moved around the table toward her, and all at once Valerie felt like a kitten being stalked by a bear. "Um—yes," she stammered, "that's the only tower around here. So—um—what did you see?"

"Oh, a number of interesting species," he continued nonchalantly. "One, in particular, enchanted me. It took a bath, then sunned itself upon a rock."

Valerie felt her face growing warm. "Oh? Which species was that?"

"Actually, it was of the pellicled variety."

"Pellicled? Which means?"

He smiled, but his dark eyes were now smoldering with sensuality as he looked her up and down. "No feathers."

Valerie's face burned. "You spied on me!"

He laughed incredulously. "Spied on you? Who took off all her clothes, then frolicked about in the full sun? Damn it, Valerie, I was worried about you."

"So that gave you the perfect excuse to be a voyeur?"

"No, not at all! I was afraid you'd gotten lost. You gave me no idea when you'd be back."

"How could I tell you when I'd be back when you weren't even speaking to me?" she practically shouted.

He held up a hand. "Okay, okay. Calm down, will you?"

But she was still seething with mortification. "Ooooh! How could you watch me like that?"

He grinned crookedly. "Binoculars, remember?"

"Oh, of all the rotten, low-down—"

He sighed. "Valerie, please—it was never my intention to spy on you. Look, I didn't intend for our conversation to go this way. Can we start over?"

She glared at him, not replying.

"I'm trying to say that I acted like an ass this morning, and I'm sorry."

Now her expression was amazed.

"Will you please cut me some slack here? Humble pie isn't exactly my long suit."

"I've noticed!"

He glanced at her starkly. "Please, will you forgive me and let's get this over with?"

She eyed him with resentment for a long moment. Then she shrugged and said primly, "Very well. We do have to work together, after all."

"That didn't sound too sincere to me," he put in reproachfully.

She raised her chin defiantly. "It's the best you're getting under the circumstances."

But he was adamantly shaking his head as he started toward her again. "No, I'm not satisfied. Let's make up."

Valerie gasped, feeling highly unsettled by the feral gleam in his eye as he stalked her. Backing off, she stammered, "Just because you saw me doesn't mean you can . . ."

"Can what, darling?" But he didn't let her reply as he quickly closed the distance between them and hauled her close.

His kiss was hard, almost bruising, as he crushed her against his solid strength. His arms trembled with the force of his need as his tongue pressed past her teeth to penetrate her mouth brazenly.

Valerie's world careered crazily. Roger's nearness was so masterful and electrifying that she could only moan and kiss him back.

After a moment, his lips moved hungrily to her cheek, her ear, her hair. "You're still damp," he said, brushing her hair aside and licking the sensitive skin beneath her ear. "You're beautiful, Valerie. Your body's beautiful. Woman, I couldn't take my eyes off you."

"Roger!"

Her cry was half a plea for mercy, half a demand for release. Then he kissed her again, and she couldn't seem to think of why this would be so wrong, or even why she was so mad at him. She just wanted an end to the tension, the terrible alienation they had both endured.

"Did you think about me while you were out there naked?" he demanded thickly, his eyes blazing down into hers. "Did you?"

"Yes," she admitted, facing him without guilt.

"What did you imagine? Tell me!"

"This," she whispered with a shudder.

He groaned and kissed her again. She stiffened slightly as he began pulling at her buttons. "Easy," he whispered, undoing the clasp on her lacy bra. He leaned over and latched his mouth onto her breast, and she gasped in ecstasy. Her nipples were already so tight that they hurt, and his wonderful lips compounded the ecstasy with an almost unbearable poignance. As he drew more of her breast into his mouth, he stuffed his hands boldly into her jeans, kneading her bottom and binding her against him. Valerie could barely catch her breath. She felt herself breaking out in gooseflesh, her hips instinctively arching against his hard arousal as a heavy, painful throbbing settled between her thighs. How she ached to feel him inside her!

"You're exquisite," he breathed as he flicked his tongue over her nipple. "Do you know I've been dying to do this since yesterday? Hell, I've been dying to do this since the moment I met you. You've got the sexiest little bottom, the sweetest breasts—"

"Roger," she gasped, shuddering violently.

"Be still," he commanded.

"But you're driving me crazy," she panted.

"Good," he whispered fiercely, his fingers digging into her softness, allowing her no retreat as his mouth continued the sweet torture.

When he straightened to kiss her again, it was her turn to rip at his shirt. She ran her fingers over his muscular chest, marveling at the dense dark hair, the hard muscles, the play of light over his skin. Looking down as he nipped at her ear, she murmured, "You have little silver hairs on your chest, there among the dark ones. They're pretty."

Roger stiffened, then broke away from Valerie so abruptly she felt as if he'd thrown ice water in her face. For a long moment, he remained still as a statue, frowning as if he'd just heard something outside. Then as she watched, trembling and appalled, he dashed for the front window, stuffing his shirt into his pants and grabbing his binoculars on the way.

"It's the Bachman's warbler!" he cried. "I'd know that song anywhere."

Without another word, he dashed out the front door.

Valerie was stunned, utterly stupefied. She simply couldn't believe that Roger had done this to her—walking out on her to chase some bird, when she was about to die from wanting him!

HE RETURNED AN HOUR LATER, looking exultant. Valerie got up from the couch, where she had sat, seething, ever since he'd left.

"I spotted him!" Roger announced triumphantly. "He and his mate are building their nest not two hundred yards from our cabin. I'll want to take you there tomorrow, so you can get some really good shots."

She said nothing.

He glanced at her sheepishly. "I'm sorry about my—er— behavior before. I didn't mean to leave you so abruptly. It's just that I've been trying to spot this bird for ten years. When I heard his call, I just had to go. You understand, don't you?"

Now it was Valerie's turn to be grouchy. "Go to hell, Roger," she snapped, walking out of the room.

8

"We have to talk about this, you know," Roger said.

"Talk about what?" Valerie asked.

It was two hours later, and Valerie and Roger were seated at the dining table, tensely eating the dinner he had prepared—she assumed, as a peace offering. The seafood quiche he had baked was delicious, with a succulent filling and a rich flaky crust. Normally Valerie would have marveled at Roger's culinary talent. However, she was hardly in a mood to be appeased.

"We're going to have to talk about what happened this afternoon," he went on.

She glanced up at him resentfully. "Nothing happened this afternoon."

"That's just what we need to talk about." As she continued to glower at him, he added with a groan, "I knew this was going to happen."

"You knew what was going to happen?"

"That this attraction we feel was going to interfere with our professional goals while we're here."

She harrumphed. "You didn't let it interfere with your professional goals in the least this afternoon, as I recall."

He gestured in supplication. "Will you give me a chance here?"

"I'm listening," she snapped back.

He sighed. "I want to explain to you about this afternoon. First, once again, I wish to apologize for my behavior. It's been a long time since I've come across like a sex-starved adolescent."

She lifted her wineglass and indolently took a sip. "Actually I rather liked the way you came across." With perverse pleasure, she heard him wince and watched a pained expression grip his normally controlled features.

He spoke in a hoarse, strained voice. "Valerie, I just want you to understand that when I bolted out of your arms, it really wasn't because of the bird calling."

Now he had her undivided attention. She set down her wineglass and stared at him. "It wasn't?"

"No." He smiled sheepishly. "Well, I did hear the song of the Bachman's warbler. But actually, nothing could have pulled me from your arms at that point, except—"

"Except?"

He glanced away and cleared his throat. "Your comment about my gray hair."

She laughed incredulously. "You've got to be kidding!"

"No, I'm not." He leaned toward her, speaking passionately. "Believe it or not, ever since we arrived here, you've been driving me crazy. I find you very attractive—in a lot of ways. And I've been trying my best to distance myself from you."

"But why?"

"I'm getting to that." He caught a ragged breath. "This would never work between us. I'm forty-five years old—a good twenty years older than you."

That bit of information took Valerie aback for a moment. She'd surmised before that Roger was at least forty. Yet he was one of those well-preserved types whose actual age was hard to figure. Now she realized that they were talking about a solid twenty-year difference between them. Nevertheless, Valerie was hardly one to judge a relationship by external criteria alone. Indeed, Roger's maturity was one aspect that had always appealed to her.

"Why should our age difference rule out our having a relationship?" she asked him bluntly.

"It's not just a difference in age. It's a difference in perspective. We don't want the same things from life."

"How do you know what I want? You've never asked me."

"Valerie, you're what? Twenty-five?"

"Yes."

"You're at the point where you want to set the world on fire with your career. Am I right?"

"Well, yes."

"And at some point, you'll want to settle down, have children. Am I in error there?"

"Well, no."

"Don't you see? I'm beyond the point where I want to pursue those things. I'm more settled, more mellowed out. My life runs at a different pace from yours. I'm looking for a more mature relationship."

"Any relationship involves compromise."

"That's true. But there still has to be a certain underlying compatibility of perspective. I just don't see it with us."

She shook her head. "Wow. That's blunt."

"I felt I owed you the truth."

"Yes. I'm rather relieved to learn that you have a closed mind about all of this." She forced a thin smile. "Except, of course, when your libido gets in the way."

He sighed again. "What happened this afternoon—it wasn't just lust. I think I could fall for you in a big way. But I feel that in the long run, it wouldn't be right. It wouldn't be fair to you."

"Not fair to me? Don't you think I should be the judge of that?" Before he could answer, she went on bitterly, "Oh, I know. You think I should bow to your more mature judgment, right? Why don't you just admit that you've never taken me seriously?"

"Oh, I've taken you seriously—believe me," he put in rue-fully. "For now, could we just be friends? I don't want to seem mercenary, but we do have a book to complete."

"I know," she said dismally.

He extended his hand across the table. "Friends?"

She took his hand. "Friends."

DURING THE NEXT FEW WEEKS, Valerie and Roger approached their relationship more as friends—at least, outwardly. Val-erie found that Roger was much less arrogant and surly these days, and he seemed more vulnerable somehow.

She often thought of the day when he had brought his feelings out into the open. She frequently considered his rea-sons for not wanting a relationship with her—the age gap between them, the differences in perspective he had men-tioned. She found that all of these things actually mattered very little to her. She wished they didn't matter so much to Roger.

Each day, she continued to feel more attracted to him, especially as the layers of his pretension were stripped away. And each day, she remained very disappointed that he wasn't willing to give them a chance.

Nevertheless, she was grateful for this smoother period between them. They enjoyed each other more, laughed to-gether more, shared experiences as friends do. The tension between them eased up in a lot of ways.

Yet it continued to build in others as they worked very closely together. Daily they went on hikes to spot warblers, and they were compiling a special section for Roger's book on the Bachman's warbler and his new family. It was hard for Valerie to stand so close to Roger, photographing the war-bler and his mate building their nest, and not think of ro-mance. Roger was evidently having a similar difficulty. One day as they worked, he inched closer to her and slipped his arm around her waist. Then he cleared his throat and whispered an instruction in her ear, evidently to cover for his momentary lapse.

This sexual pull continued to intensify despite Roger's efforts to fight it. It came out in little ways. When he touched Valerie out in the woods to help her spot a bird, she could hear his breathing quicken. Or when they sipped a glass of wine before dinner and discussed the discoveries they'd made that day, Roger's eyes would suddenly darken—with pride and something far deeper—as they swept over her. When they exchanged secretive, longing glances...

When it became so hard to say good-night, for him to climb up to the loft, for her to go off to her lonely bunk.

Early one morning, as Valerie left her bedroom, she practically collided with Roger just outside her door. She was wearing a negligee and peignoir, he was wearing only his pajama bottoms. As they both jumped back to avoid impact, she stared at his sexy tousled hair, the strong muscles of his hair-covered chest. He in turn devoured her disheveled hair, her lush curves peeking through the sheer fabric of her nightclothes. There was such a sexual hunger blazing in his eyes, she was surprised that her gown and peignoir didn't erupt into flames. And she dared not even look below his waist, because she was certain of what she would see!

Then Roger abruptly coughed, muttered, "Excuse me," and walked out the front door in his pajama bottoms and bare feet—going where, she had no idea. And she was certain Roger didn't have the foggiest grasp of his destination, either. It would have been downright ludicrous had she not felt so frustrated!

They went into Meadville several times, to get new hiking boots and to send Valerie's film off to her father in Natchez. Although Fred Vernon had not been delighted about Valerie's going to the woods with Roger, he had promised to develop her slides and send them back to her in care of the national forest.

Soon the color slides started coming back, and Roger was delighted with Valerie's work. He was astonished at the number of warblers she'd managed to capture and made it clear that he thought her photography was top-notch. He complimented her on the crispness and balance of her images, her dramatic usage of light and shadow.

They spent much time together labeling the slides and choosing the best ones for possible inclusion in Roger's book. One day, after they'd screened and labeled over a hundred slides, Roger remarked, "You know, after Rico was injured, I had grave misgivings about finishing this project on time. But you've really saved it for me, Valerie." Shaking his head, he added, "Your abilities are uncanny. You are truly gifted."

Valerie was so overwhelmed by his ardent compliment that she blushed. "Aren't you exaggerating a bit?"

"No, I'm not. Just wait until my publisher sees some of these shots. You know, Amory mentioned to me that he and his wife are coming to Natchez on a vacation in a few weeks— although actually, I think he's coming this way to check on our progress on the book. He's been very concerned about this project ever since Rico broke his leg. The publication date for the book is pretty firmly fixed, as I understand it. Anyway, if Amory does come to Natchez, I want you to meet him, Valerie."

"I'd be delighted," she said eagerly.

"I know that when he sees your work, he'll want you to do other assignments for him."

"That's so generous of you."

He shrugged. "I told you that if you'd help me rescue this project, I'd help you get launched. And I meant it."

She had to laugh. "You know you've come a long way from that day when we met at my dad's photography shop."

"Indeed, I have." He stared at her meaningfully and she back at him, and both knew that his remark went far beyond photography.

9

As THE WEEKS PASSED, Valerie developed a casual friendship with Helen Broussard of Broussard's Store. They saw the friendly widow often when they went back to the highway for supplies.

It was during their fourth week in the forest that Helen invited them to a gathering she was hosting. Valerie was visiting with Helen at the counter that day while Roger searched for some hardware supplies. The back door out at the cabin kept sticking, and he was determined to fix it.

"Why don't you folks come join us tonight. We're having a little family gathering behind the store," Helen told Valerie.

"Why, that's so kind of you," Valerie replied with a smile. "But I'd hate to intrude on your family."

Helen waved her off. "Honey, just about everyone around these parts is my family. Won't you come?"

"Well, it does sound delightful. I'll have to check with Roger, though."

Just then, Roger approached the counter with a plane and a set of hinges he'd selected. He swallowed hard as he stared at Valerie leaning on the counter with her derriere displayed temptingly. Tight jeans again—the girl seemed to live in them. Somehow he'd managed to keep his hands off her during these past few weeks, but it hadn't been easy!

She turned, straightening as he approached, and the loveliness of her face, the sparkle in her eyes, had him inwardly groaning. The T-shirt she wore—emblazoned with *North-*

east Louisiana University—reminded him of her youthfulness. The places where it clung to her so seductively reminded him of a far darker emotion.

"Helen has invited us to a party tonight," she told him with a smile.

"We often have little community supper dances in the pavilion behind the store," Helen explained to Roger, "and we'd love to have you folks join us tonight."

"Thanks, Helen," Roger murmured stiffly as he set down his supplies. "But I'm not sure we can make it. The rest of the day is pretty well booked for Valerie and me."

As Valerie shot Roger a perturbed glance, Helen waved him off and said, "Look, folks, come if you can, okay? You don't need to send us no formal acceptance—just show up."

The two again thanked Helen for the invitation, and Valerie promised that they'd come if they could.

In the car going back to the forest, Valerie asked Roger, "Why don't you want to go to Helen's gathering tonight?"

He gripped the steering wheel tightly, not wanting to tell her that the idea of holding her in his arms again—even if to dance—was driving him crazy. "We do have a schedule to maintain, Valerie."

She laughed shortly. "We can't watch birds at night."

"Ah, but you can continue studying my bird guides, and I can complete my notes for the day."

She sighed. "I suppose you're right. I just thought it might be nice to get out of the cabin for a change."

He didn't answer as he turned the car into the entrance to the national forest.

BACK AT THE CABIN, they unloaded their supplies, then Valerie helped Roger take down the back door. They dragged two dining chairs outside and laid the door across them. Valerie steadied the door as Roger planed it. Watching him work, his expression frowningly intent, she said, "My, you're rather handy around the house, Mr. Benedict."

He grunted. "I do a lot of my own repair work at my house in Westbury."

She chuckled. "You know, you have a lot of nice qualities, fella. You're a pretty mean cook, and you don't mind helping out around the place. I'm surprised some woman with bad plumbing and squeaky doors hasn't grabbed you."

"Oh, I'm a pretty slippery character," he assured her. But he turned away to hide a self-satisfied grin.

After they had rehung the door, which now fit perfectly, Valerie stifled a yawn. Observing her, Roger said, "Why don't you take a nap this afternoon while I go for a hike alone?"

She nodded, finding she suddenly did feel quite sleepy. "Guess I did get up awfully early for my hike this morning," she remarked. "And I do have a few things to do around the cabin, so if you don't mind—"

"Not at all," he replied with a stiff smile.

Valerie went back inside the cabin, and Roger gathered his gear and hiked out alone, grateful for the respite away from her. At first he tried spotting birds, but soon lost interest and merely walked briskly over the warm, rolling terrain. Despite his best efforts, however, he just couldn't get his mind off Valerie. He shook his head as he remembered her leaning on the counter at Helen's store, looking so damn cute in her T-shirt and jeans.

He was having a hard time sticking to their commitment to keep their relationship platonic, just as he sensed that she was having a similar difficulty. In so many ways, Valerie was a delight to have around. She was bright, quick, a wonderful conversationalist. And she was so talented. The pride he took in her accomplishments was deepening into something far more profound, far more threatening.

And she was so very sexy. There was an unconsciousness, almost an innocence, about her allure. The girl often enticed him without even seeming to know it. Like that morning when they'd almost collided outside her door, he in his pajama bottoms and she in that wispy little peignoir and gown. Even now, he groaned at the memory. The sight of her had aroused him so, he'd stumbled out the front door of the cabin, and he'd been fifty yards down the trail before he'd realized that he'd made a complete ass of himself. At least a dozen times each day, she continued to drive him crazy—when he caught the scent of her perfume or watched her brush her thick auburn hair or saw her sweet nothings fluttering on the clothesline outside. Especially then.

And the longing glances she often sent his way told him that she found him appealing, too. Like any male animal, Roger couldn't contain a feeling of immense pride that such a young, beautiful woman desired him. Yet to take what she offered—he still couldn't get beyond the fact that it would be wrong. She deserved someone who could fulfill her youthful expectations.

Of course, that noble conclusion failed to make him want her any less!

He hiked out far, trying to vent his growing frustration. A light rain began to fall, but even that didn't cool down the hard knot of desire that never seemed to leave him. . . .

WHEN ROGER RETURNED to the cabin late that afternoon, he was damp and still feeling frustrated. He shelved his equipment in the back room then started toward the kitchen. Unfortunately, he wasn't really looking where he was going, and when he stepped into the kitchen, his face slammed smack into a damp blue satin bra, which was strung up, with half a dozen other lacy unmentionables, on a nylon line across the room. He jumped back as if burned, bellowing a string of oaths that brought Valerie rushing in within seconds.

Yet when he watched her appear across from him in the dining area, he was sorry he'd ever opened his mouth. He peered at her through the narrow slit between her bra and an equally naughty-looking pair of panties dangling next to it. Obviously, Valerie had just gotten out of bed—her hair was sensually mussed, and she was wearing only her T-shirt, panties and socks, a very short terry robe thrown across her shoulders. Her long, bare legs were exquisite, especially as she stood there near the window, the light playing over her lovely youthful skin. She looked breathtakingly beautiful. And sexy as hell!

"Roger, are you all right?" she asked sleepily.

He batted the bra out of the way as he stepped forward. "I can't even get through the damned kitchen—it's booby-trapped!" he barked out. Then, realizing what he'd just said, he turned away to hide the hot color rising in his face.

"I'm sorry," he heard her say defensively. "It was raining and I didn't have anywhere else to hang my hand washables."

He glanced at her quickly and realized she looked hurt and confused by his lambasting. What a jerk he was, he chided himself. She'd obviously been sound asleep, and he'd not only rudely awakened her, here he was bellowing at her about something that was not at all her fault.

"No, I'm the one who must apologize," he said quickly and awkwardly. "I woke you up, didn't I?"

She nodded unsteadily. "It's all right. I needed to get up, anyway."

Roger stifled a miserable groan. She looked so damn sweet and vulnerable standing across from him. He knew that any moment now, he'd take her into his arms and then...heaven help them both. He turned away and gripped the counter violently. "Let's go to Helen's party," he said hoarsely.

At once her tone brightened. "Do you mean it?"

He didn't dare turn around to look at her. "Sure. Let's just get ready and go. As quickly as possible."

"Fine," she said behind him.

He turned, breathing a sigh of relief as he watched her walk off. Suddenly the idea of getting out of the cabin appealed greatly to Roger Benedict.

TWILIGHT WAS APPROACHING by the time they drove back to Meadville. Valerie had brought along to the woods only one dress—a casual peach-colored jersey—and she wore it tonight with a festive string of white beads and matching sandals. She wore her hair down in curls about her neck and shoulders, and she caught Roger glancing at her appreciatively as they drove along. He looked just as appealing to her, dressed in dark slacks and a plaid sports shirt.

There was quite a line of cars and pickup trucks in the parking lot of Helen's store, and Roger eased the car beneath a tree at the side of the road. He helped Valerie out, then they walked toward the pavilion behind the store, listening to the humming of cicadas, the hooting of a barred owl and the distant sounds of revelry.

At least a dozen families were gathered under the pavilion, which was strung with colorful lights. The scene was alive with music, laughter and the enticing smells of home-cooked foods. Honeysuckle, curling riotously on the latticework, added its special fragrance to the balmy night air. On a small platform at one end of the pavilion, three elderly musicians—two fiddlers and an accordion player—played music with a distinctively Cajun flavor, completing the homespun ambience.

They'd no sooner arrived at the edge of the pavilion than Helen rushed up to greet them, wearing a blue jean skirt and a cheerful checked blouse. "So glad you folks made it, after all."

Valerie nodded toward the array of covered dishes laid out on a nearby table. "We didn't think to bring anything. I'm embarrassed."

"Now, don't you be embarrassed, 'cause I didn't ask you to bring nothing," Helen replied stoutly. "You're our guests this evening."

Helen introduced Valerie and Roger to the families, all of whom were related to the storekeeper in one way or another. A few of the families ran farms, while others had husbands employed by oil or forestry companies. Some of the wives worked in local shops or offices, while others stayed home to raise small children. Both Roger and Valerie enjoyed the uniquely old-fashioned atmosphere, complete with extended families.

They ate dinner with Helen, her son, Claude, his wife and three small children. The food ranged from Southern favorites such as chicken and dumplings, country ham and potato salad, to more traditional Cajun dishes such as catfish stew, *boudin* sausage and barbecued quail.

All of the Broussards were intensely curious about the book Valerie and Roger were working on, and the subject of bird-watching commanded most of the conversation during the meal. Claude was particularly interested in Roger's book, since he was a farmer and got to see many different species of birds as he made his daily rounds. "There's one bird I see quite often down by the creek," he told Roger. "It's the prettiest thing I've ever seen—no bigger than a sparrow, but bright red, blue and green."

"It's a painted bunting," Roger informed him eagerly. "And it is, indeed, one of our most spectacular species."

"Why don't you come out to the farm and see it before you leave the area?" Claude suggested.

"I'd love to," Roger replied.

The younger Broussards had an ebullient eighteen-month-old baby, and after dinner Helen held the child while her son and daughter-in-law went out to the dance floor. The couple's older children—a boy about six and a girl around five—also went out to dance, holding hands as they swayed about with their parents. Watching the two children, Valerie smiled. Then, hearing a delightful gurgle, she turned to watch the baby flail his arms and coo up at Roger, who was sitting across from him. Roger winked at the baby then told Helen, "Quite a lusty little grandson you have there."

"He keeps these old bones active," she replied with a grin, shifting the baby on her lap. Eyeing Roger and Valerie sternly, she added, "Now why aren't you two out there dancing with the others?"

Roger glanced at Valerie sheepishly. He'd been dreading this moment, remembering the sweet torture of dancing with her on the *Delta Princess*. Tonight she looked equally delicious sitting next to him, dressed in that clingy peach-coloured dress and wearing some sweet, seductive perfume.

"Want to dance?" he asked.

"Thought you'd never ask," she replied.

Hand in hand, they went out onto the dance floor. Roger took Valerie into his arms, and they swayed about to the singsongy music of fiddle and accordion. He swallowed hard as he inhaled the fresh essence of her hair. As always she felt slim and quite wonderful in his embrace. Why did he foolishly assume that getting out of the cabin would lessen his sexual frustration? He had taken his problem along with him—and what a lovely problem she was!

After a while he couldn't resist saying, "I've been wondering something, Valerie."

She looked up at him, her blue-violet eyes lovely in the soft light. "Yes?"

He cleared his throat, feeling as if he were about to plunge off a steep cliff, but unable to contain the impulse driving him. "When I came in this afternoon and woke you up, I hurt your feelings, didn't I?" he asked.

She pressed her face against his shoulder, and his heart welled at the tender, trusting gesture. "Yes," she admitted in a small voice.

Roger couldn't stop the hand that now slipped beneath her hair, stroking the back of her neck to comfort her. "Why, darling?"

"You barked at me," she said.

"Yes, I know I did, but I mean . . ." He paused, smiling self-deprecatingly. "We both know that it's hardly the first time I've started bellowing. Why did it get to you this time?"

She was quiet a minute, then pulled back and said earnestly, "I guess because we've become such good friends. I thought we were beyond that sort of thing, you shouting at me and all."

He groaned and clutched her to him tightly, feeling his arms tremble about her. "I'm so damn sorry." In an unsteady voice, he added, "But do you have any idea what it does to a man—seeing your sweet nothings strung up all over the place?"

"It's not my fault that it was raining, and I was out of underwear."

"Out of underwear," he repeated with an agonized moan, clutching her even tighter. "I can't think of what unsettles me more, the image of you with your underwear . . . or without it."

She drew back, chuckling. "Roger, that's wicked."

The music stopped and for a moment they merely stared at each other. Then Roger cleared his throat and said awkwardly, "Come on. Let's get some more punch and go find Helen's son. I need to get instructions to his farm. He promised to take me bird-watching this Saturday."

"Sure," she said with a smile.

AFTER DANCING WITH ROGER, Valerie was euphoric. She'd felt hurt earlier when he'd snapped at her, but now she understood that when he'd lashed out at her, it was only because he'd desired her and had been fighting himself about it.

Well, he couldn't keep fighting himself forever, she thought with perverse satisfaction. She certainly couldn't fight the attraction she felt for him. Every day Roger Benedict grew more human and endeared himself to her more.

She thoroughly enjoyed the evening—enjoyed being with Roger and visiting with Helen and her family. The punch they drank was laced with wine, and while Roger had only one more round, Valerie indulged herself with several more cupfuls. It had been a long time since she'd gotten even slightly tipsy, and tonight she felt like celebrating this lovely occasion and the new intimacy she and Roger had achieved.

They danced together several more times. A couple of other men asked her to dance, too, and while Roger at first voiced no objection, she was pleasantly surprised when he broke in as she danced with Claude. With a grin, Claude turned Valerie back over to Roger.

"Why, Roger, I'm overwhelmed," she told him as he pulled her into his arms none too gently.

He harrumphed. "You looked a little too happy out there with Claude."

She feigned amazement. "My, my. Are we jealous?"

"Of course not."

"Then don't you want me to be happy?" she teased.

"You're supposed to be my date tonight."

She felt a keen thrill at his possessive tone, the smoldering look in his eyes. "You mean we're actually having a date?"

"It's the principle of the thing," he said self-righteously.

But she knew, as he drew her closer, that it was far more than the principle of the thing....

Later, as they took a break and again chatted with Helen, the baby kept making eyes at Roger. Roger thoroughly enjoyed the tyke and soon offered to take the baby so Helen could have a break. Roger settled the child in his lap, and the baby promptly fell asleep, his little head, with its riot of black curls, nestled trustingly against Roger's arm. Studying the two of them, Valerie felt quite touched. She'd never before imagined Roger with a baby, but he handled Helen's grandson like a real pro. She remembered his saying once that he had wanted children during his marriage, but his wife hadn't.

Then she remembered him telling her recently that he was beyond the stage in life where he wanted children. Still he looked surprisingly content with the baby in his lap.

When the gathering began to break up, Helen's daughter-in-law came to take the baby from Roger. Watching Roger hand over the child, Helen smiled at him and Valerie and said, "You know, you two make a mighty fine couple."

Roger winked at Valerie, then told Helen solemnly, "Actually, since I've met Valerie, I've been tempted more than once to rob the cradle."

Feeling delighted by his teasing, Valerie set down her punch cup and took his arm. "Speaking of which, I guess it's time for us to leave, Helen. It's past Roger's bedtime, you see."

Roger shot Valerie a stern glance and quipped back, "Yes, I believe I'd best get this youngster home. She's made one too many trips to the punch bowl tonight."

The two thanked Helen and left. Valerie felt supremely happy as she and Roger walked off hand in hand. He wasn't being so defensive about the age gap between them, she realized. They could actually laugh about it now.

WHEN THEY ENTERED THE CABIN a few minutes later, Valerie was humming one of the lilting Cajun melodies they had danced to.

"You're a little tipsy, my dear," Roger remarked as he turned on the light.

"S'okay," she replied, smiling at him crookedly. "I wasn't driving, remember?"

He coughed. "I think you'd better go on to bed."

"What if I need your help?" she asked wickedly.

"Valerie," he cautioned as she started toward him.

"I was just thinking about what you said, Roger."

"Yes?"

"About robbing the cradle."

"Yes?"

She stepped up to him, giggled and wrapped her arms around his neck. "Well . . . rob away."

He groaned, glancing down at her with both tenderness and frustration. "I would never rob a lady who is not in full possession of her faculties."

"Oh, I don't care," she said recklessly, and kissed him.

When he pulled away, he was breathing hard and gripping her shoulders with fingers that trembled. "You're forgetting that we agreed to be friends."

"Maybe I want to amend our agreement." She stretched on tiptoe, running her tongue boldly over his lower lip.

"Amend, hell," he said thickly, again holding her at bay with his hands. "If we should ever get together—"

"If?" she repeated gleefully. "You mean there's actually an 'if' now?"

He continued forbearingly. "If we should ever get together, you're going to remember every minute of it, lady."

"What if I promise to take notes?" she asked impishly.

He whacked her fanny. "Go to bed, little siren, before I abandon my better judgment."

"You're always so in control, aren't you Roger?" she asked petulantly.

"Wanna bet?" he growled. Before she could respond, he pointed to her bedroom and said, "Now, scoot."

She started off, shooting him a resentful glance.

Roger sighed raggedly as he switched off the light. The hardest thing he'd ever done was to climb up into the loft alone. The night seemed interminable as he gazed up at the stars through the skylight and thought of her, yearned for her to be there beside him.

He knew it was only a matter of time before they wound up in each other's arms again. What was he going to do?

THE INEVITABLE HAPPENED a couple days later, while they were hiking out in the woods. It was late afternoon and they were heading back toward the cabin. They were laughing, discussing the antics of two blue jays they'd spotted bickering with a mockingbird.

Valerie was leading them down the now-familiar trail they'd established. She called back to Roger, "I can't believe how ludicrous those birds sounded as they blessed each other out. Why, they were almost hu—"

Then abruptly Roger lunged forward, caught Valerie about the waist and pulled her back violently against a tree.

She gasped, "What the—"

Yet he silenced her by clamping a hand over her mouth. He nodded toward the trail. Glancing ahead, Valerie quickly surmised why he had grabbed her. Right where she'd been about to step, a big, fat copperhead snake slithered across the path.

"Oh, God," she muttered as he released her mouth, tottering so badly that Roger had to hold her tight to keep her from collapsing.

"Are you all right?" he asked tensely.

She nodded, then said convulsively, "I almost s-stepped on a copperhead."

"He's just out looking for a rock to warm himself on," Roger explained. "Though I doubt he would have appreciated being stepped on. Good thing we're wearing our snake leggings."

She tottered again, and he caught her to him, scanning her face anxiously. "Good grief, Valerie, you're as white as a ghost." He gently removed her camera and binoculars and set them, with his equipment, at their feet. Then he unbuttoned the top two buttons on her blouse, resting his fingertips just above her breasts. His eyes flashed simultaneously with alarm, concern, desire. "Do you realize how hard your heart is beating?"

"Yes," she replied, her voice having a hollow, tinny ring.

"Why were you so frightened?"

She drew a convulsive breath and said, "When I was ten, my parents took me camping, and I insisted on having my own pup tent. Anyway, to make a long story short, there was evidently a hole in my tent, and I woke up the next morning to find a big black snake curled up next to me."

"What did you do?"

"I screamed my head off, of course, and Dad came running and killed the snake. As it turned out, it wasn't poisonous, but after that—"

"I understand," Roger said gently. He nestled Valerie closer, yet his hand remained inside her shirt, touching her possessively. "You poor darling. You mean, you're terrified of snakes and still you came out here with me?"

As he pulled back to wait for her reply, she looked up at him starkly and said, "I happen to believe that fears and stumbling blocks are made to be overcome."

For a moment they merely stared at each other, an emotion very profound passing between them. His eyes glowed as he replied, "You would believe that. You're so young and so brave."

As they continued to stare at each other, his fingers slipped inside her bra, caressing the nipple of her breast, which was now hard, aching for his touch. She moaned and pressed herself into his fingers as his eyes continued to search hers.

"Don't worry, darling. I'm not going to let anything happen to you."

"Good," she murmured, loving the feel of his rough fingers on her sensitive nipple. She forced a crooked smile. "Well, I must say that for someone of your advanced years, you move pretty fast, Mr. Benedict."

"Watch this."

His mouth caught hers hungrily as he pinned her against the tree. She kissed him back as his fingertips squeezed her nipple. She felt so protected, so cherished, in his embrace. He was truly her friend now, and she wanted him as her lover. His arousal was pressing insistently against her, driving her crazy in a highly pleasurable way. She insinuated a hand between them to touch him boldly, to establish her own possession.

Almost violently he pulled himself away from her. Standing with his back to her, he clenched his fists and said, "I'm sorry, Valerie. So damn sorry."

"You're sorry? How do you think I feel?" Valerie's voice seethed with frustration as she gathered her equipment then started back down the trail. "This isn't working, Roger! It just isn't working!"

10

EARLY THE NEXT AFTERNOON, they headed for Meadville to buy film. On their way out of the park, the ranger stopped them, handing Valerie a package of slides her father had just sent her.

They ran errands in town and planned to do their laundry before returning to the forest. But first they stopped for a late lunch at a local restaurant they'd spotted, a homey little place with chintz curtains and cozy booths.

As they perused their menus, Valerie kept catching Roger staring at her. He'd been trying his best to pretend that their passionate interlude in the forest had never occurred. Yet his eyes told a different story. They couldn't seem to resist roving over her again and again, both last night and today. They touched her with an intimacy as intense and burning as his hands, his lips, had been.

Valerie knew that the barriers were crumbling between them, even if Roger Benedict was determined to kick and scream every step of the way!

A few minutes later, as they were eating their delicious down-home plate lunches, Roger patted his stomach and said, "It's been some time since I've had Southern fried chicken complete with cream gravy. All we need now are mint juleps."

Valerie laughed. "You know, Roger, not every Southerner comes straight from the pages of *Gone With the Wind*. I've never had a mint julep in my life."

"Never?"

She chuckled. "Well, maybe once or twice."

He cut a morsel of breast meat and dipped it in gravy. "This is luscious, every bit as good as the food at Helen's gathering the other night. It's a good thing we don't eat in town every day, or I'd leave Mississippi ten pounds heavier."

She smiled. "You don't look like you have a problem with your weight."

"Ha! I'm twenty pounds heavier than I was as a young man."

"Then you must have been quite a rail back then. The weight looks good on you. You're very—" she eyed him appreciatively "—solid."

"Well, I've really had to fight to keep from getting a gut."

"You've succeeded," she replied.

They continued to chat over their food. Toward the end of the meal, Roger said, "I've been wondering something, Valerie."

"Yes?"

"I hate to sound nosy, but my curiosity is getting the better of me."

"Oh?"

"When you opened the box of slides in the car, wasn't there a note from your dad inside?"

Valerie laughed. "You're very observant."

"But you didn't read it. You just slipped it into your purse."

She nodded. "Dad sends me a note each week with the slides."

Roger smiled. "He does? Then why didn't you . . . ? Look, if I'm being too inquisitive here—"

"No, you're not." She set down her fork. "If I didn't read Dad's note, it's only because I already know what he has to say."

He laughed. "You do?"

Meeting his amused gaze, she dramatized, "'Dear Valerie, I miss you and hope you'll come home soon. Customers keep asking for you at the shop—not that I'm having *any* difficulty handling everything on my own....'" As Roger chuckled, she paused to take the note from her purse, read it silently, then added, "Yep, I just about hit the nail on the head. Except for this: 'By the way, Mr. Sears called from the high school wanting to know if you'll do the graduation pictures as usual this year.'" She sighed. "A new twist."

Roger was shaking his head. "Your dad wants you home."

"No lie."

He coughed and said awkwardly, "Well, we only have a couple more weeks of work to do here."

"Right," Valerie acknowledged tightly. "Then I'll go home, you'll go back to New York, and everything will be just fine, won't it, Roger?"

They stared at each other in the painful silence that fell in the wake of her words. Then the waitress came up, gathering their dishes and asking them if they'd like some dessert. "It's peach cobbler today," she told Roger with a friendly smile.

"It sounds divine," he replied, "but I'm afraid I've already done enough damage for one meal. Valerie?"

"I'd like just coffee, please."

"Two coffees, then," Roger said.

Valerie looked preoccupied as the waitress left, and Roger asked, "Something wrong? Still thinking of your dad?"

"Guess I am," she admitted. "And I was just remembering that my mom used to make the best peach cobbler in Natchez."

"Oh, did she? Shall I call the waitress back?"

"No, thanks. It wouldn't be the same."

He was studying her intently. "Why don't you tell me about your mother?"

"Sure," she replied with a brave smile. "Mom was a wonderful person—very lively, very kind. She was basically a homemaker, although she was also involved with the local historical society and sometimes served as a tour guide at some of our antebellum mansions. She was great to me— baked me cookies, sewed for me, sponsored my Girl Scout troop."

"You had a great childhood, then."

She nodded and felt a tear stinging. "The best."

The waitress arrived with their coffee, and after they began sipping the rich brew, Roger went on, "Do you want to tell me what happened—last year when your mother died?"

Valerie set down her coffee cup. "It was a series of strokes. You see, Mom had chronic kidney disease, which resulted in high blood pressure. We had thought she was doing so well, although she often pretended to be doing better than she actually was. Then…" She sighed heavily. "She was only fifty-seven when she died."

He reached out to cover her trembling hand with his own. "I'm so sorry, Valerie."

"It was hard. Even harder because—"

"Yes?"

She withdrew her hand from his, clearing her throat. "I was engaged once."

He looked taken aback. "You were?"

She nodded. "It wasn't that long ago, but it seems like forever, somehow. I was twenty-three, Mark twenty-four. Everything was fine until Mark lost his job in the oil industry. Then he decided to compensate by dumping me and marrying into a wealthy family."

"What a jerk," Roger said.

Valerie sighed. "Mark was immature. I can recognize that now. But what was really hard was that soon after he married, he started calling me again, telling me that his marriage was a mistake and that he wanted to see me again. Of course, he never mentioned anything about possibly getting a divorce."

"You didn't see him, did you?" Roger asked.

Valerie smiled at him. "No, of course I didn't. But what was hardest of all was that Mark's calls really intensified about the time my mother became gravely ill."

"What a jackass," Roger said.

"I finally threatened to call his wife, and that was the end of his calls."

"Good for you," Roger said. He gazed at her with both tenderness and sympathy. "Poor darling. I bet it's been hard for you to trust men since then."

She set down her coffee cup and stared him straight in the eye. "I trust you."

He turned away with a groan. "You really shouldn't trust me."

"But I do." Her feelings burst forth in a rush. "And I think you're the one who's afraid to take a chance again, not me."

"That's not true," he said vehemently, turning to face her. "I got over my failed marriage a long time ago. But I will admit that I'm not willing to risk making the same mistake of committing to someone who's totally different from me."

"Why are we so different?" she demanded. "And if you say it's this age business again, I want you to know that I think that's a crock."

He laughed. "Do you, now?"

"Yes. It's only an excuse for you to avoid getting involved with me."

He leaned forward and spoke intensely. "I've tried to explain this before. It's not just the age gap between us, but the essential differences it represents."

"Such as?"

He couldn't resist a smile as he studied her. "Such as the fact that you're so young and spontaneous. And I'm so stodgy and set in my ways."

"Maybe I like you stodgy."

He shook his head, his expression miserably torn. "Valerie, I just feel you'll be better off with one of your contemporaries."

"Like?"

"Well, someone like Rico. The two of you got along much better than you and I do. He's more your age."

"Aha!" she said. "I knew you were mad the day all three of us had lunch together."

"I wasn't the least bit angry."

"Oh, yes, you were." Smiling at him, she said, "If I got along better with Rico, it was simply because there was no tension between us. No attraction."

"Speak for yourself. I'm not so sure about Rico."

She laughed. "You were jealous!"

"No, I wasn't."

"Oh, yes, you were. And still are, as a matter of fact."

"Very well, perhaps I was. Am. A little," he admitted reluctantly.

She was grinning. "Here you claim our relationship is going nowhere, and yet you're jealous."

"Well, whoever said this battle of the sexes is logical," he grumbled.

She stared at him earnestly. "Instead of always thinking of how different we are, why not start thinking of all the things we have in common? It seems to me that we've gotten along very well these past few weeks. We've really enjoyed working and just being together."

"We've managed to effect some workable compromises," he conceded. "But I still feel that in the long run, you'd be better off with—"

"I'm trying to tell you that I've had a relationship with one of my contemporaries," she cut in passionately. "I didn't care for it. And I like the fact that you're more mature and settled. Trustworthy."

He clenched his fists on the tabletop. "Once again, you shouldn't trust me."

"Why?" Lowering her voice, she demanded, "Because you want me for sex and nothing more?"

His head shot up. "Of course not!" he denied, his eyes blazing with righteous anger. "But you know my feelings about our having a future together. And you just don't seem to realize how much you'd be giving up."

"Oh, damn it, Roger," she said with a gesture of exasperation. "For all we know, you could outlive me. I could die young like Mom did, then wouldn't you feel silly."

All at once, Valerie paused, for Roger had turned white as she spoke.

"Do the doctors think—"

She quickly shook her head. "All Mom's problems began with an acute infection years ago. The doctors told my father there's no reason to believe her illness will affect me."

He sighed his relief, gazing at her starkly. "I hate the thought of anything happening to you."

"But you're still not going to give us a chance, are you?"

"Darling, I'm just afraid this won't work," he said poignantly.

This time, she was the one who reached out and touched his hand. "We'll never know unless we try, will we?"

He clutched her hand tightly in his, and they exchanged a look of anguish, a look of desire.

ON THE WAY HOME, they stopped at the local Laundromat to wash their bedding and clothes. They were quiet there and on their way back to the forest. Yet back at the cabin, as Roger viewed the new slides in a hand viewer, he couldn't contain his excited, proud reaction. "Wow! You've captured five new species!" he announced proudly to Valerie. "And this photography is superb. I wish I could take you with me on my next—"

He stopped in midsentence, and they stared at each other in miserable silence. "But you wouldn't want to leave your father," he added at last, turning away to place another slide in the viewer.

What could she say? Valerie asked herself sadly. Roger had issued a statement of fact, not a question.

Valerie got up, took her pillowcase full of clean laundry and went to her bedroom. She made up her bunk with clean sheets, then methodically began folding her clothes and replacing them in her suitcase on the upper bunk. Her time with Roger was coming to an end, she thought dismally, and this was something they were both recognizing with an underlying pain. They had drawn so close during the past weeks, had become such good friends.

Yet still, Roger maintained that there could never be anything serious between them. He cared for her in his way, but he was determined not to give in.

She cared for him, too. No, she amended, she didn't just care for him, she was coming to love him. As she'd told him earlier at lunch, she liked everything about him—the fact that he was mature and settled. Even his crustiness, his stodginess. And she hated their time together to come to an end without exploring that love, expressing it, giving it a chance....

Then maybe she'd have to accept him on his own terms, she thought, love him for today without expecting anything more. He was worth it, she decided. He just needed a nudge in the right direction.

"Valerie, come have a glass of wine with me," she heard him call out from the living room.

She smiled. They'd gotten in the habit of having a glass of wine together about five each afternoon, and it pleased her that he didn't want to go ahead without her. His possessive remarks at lunch had pleased her, too.

"Be there in just a minute," she called out.

Laying her folded clothes into her suitcase, she thoughtfully fingered the edge of the cutoffs Roger had objected to so violently the first day they came here. What was it he'd said? Ah, yes: "Wear those cutoffs again and you won't be wearing them for long." She smiled as she also recalled his intense, heated reaction to seeing her underwear strung across the kitchen a few days ago.

Perhaps it was time to give those cutoffs a try again, she thought with perverse pleasure. Roger was always so in charge, so in control—except when she got to him. And didn't she know just how to do that by now?

After she undressed and took care of the necessary precautions, she donned her panties and the cutoffs. For good measure, she put on the thinnest, tightest tank top she owned.

She pulled out a hand mirror and drew it up and down over her body. She was being brazen, but right now, it felt just fine.

When she walked back into the living room, she spotted Roger before he saw her. He was seated on the couch beyond her, about to take a sip of white wine.

She cleared her throat and he glanced up at her. He swallowed hard and almost dropped his wineglass. His eyes literally devoured her, a muscle twitched in his jaw, and when he managed to set down his glass, he did so with trembling fingers. Then he lurched unsteadily to his feet.

"You're wearing those cutoffs again." The words came out hoarse, strangled.

"I sure am," she repeated with a sultry smile. "And what are you going to do about it, fella?"

He gestured in supplication. "Oh, Valerie. Please don't do this to me. Not again."

Yet she kept coming closer.

"Valerie, please—"

Yet still she kept coming, and with an anguished groan, Roger reached out and pulled her into his arms. His kiss was wild and torrid as his hands slid possessively down her body.

His eyes blazed down into hers as he began unzipping her cutoffs.

"I warned you," he said.

Valerie shuddered as her cutoffs hit the floor. Then Roger was kissing her again, and his hands were inside her panties, his fingers roughly kneading her bare bottom as he arched her against the very hard front of him. She could feel the tension, the raging need in his body—now all unleashed on her. And she loved it!

"I warned you," he repeated intensely a moment later. "A man can only take so much...."

"It's okay," she whispered back, looking up into his eyes. "You don't have to promise me forever. I just want to be close to you."

His reply was inarticulate, although his hands spoke eloquently of his desire as his fingers dug into her hips even more insistently, sending a flame of need shooting straight to the core of her. His kiss was hot and brazen; his tongue slid deeply into her mouth. She reeled, loving his boldness, aching to feel him inside her.

He moved back slightly to stare at her unabashedly. "You're so lovely," he murmured, stroking her breasts through her tank top.

As she struggled to breathe, he raised her tank top up over the breasts that now ached to be freed, to be touched directly by his hands. But he didn't remove her top, which somehow made her feel even more vulnerable to him—especially as he stood before her fully clothed, staring at her with such devouring desire.

He leaned over to take her taut nipple in his mouth. She shuddered and said, "Roger, I just want you to know that I don't sleep around. This is very special to me."

"You think it isn't to me?" he asked passionately, flicking his tongue over her nipple. "Believe me, darling, I've been careful, too. I know it's been a while for us both."

Catching a convulsive breath, she ran her fingers through his hair and said, "I know it seems like forever since we met. I've wanted you so badly, Roger."

At her words, he straightened, his eyes burning down into hers as his manhood pressed against her pelvis. Touching her cheek, he asked hoarsely, "Darling, are you . . . ? I wouldn't want to get you pregnant."

"I'll admit that I came prepared," she said with a smile. "Guess I knew this was going to happen."

"Guess I knew it, too," he murmured back, "although I refused to acknowledge it consciously." His teeth nipped her neck as his hands lifted her buttocks to press her more intimately into him.

"Oh, Roger." She almost collapsed as his fingers stole around to her front, pressing between her thighs.

"I want you so," he whispered, and she felt her panties slip to the floor.

He stroked her for a long moment, kissing her deeply, and soon they were clawing at each other, losing control. They just made it to the couch, where he fell back with her on top of him. She ripped his shirt open as she straddled him. He caressed her bare legs and stared unabashedly at the intimate places now revealed before him. She impatiently unbuckled his belt then undid his jeans.

As he began bringing them together, she reached downward and touched him boldly, then grinned at him appreciatively. "Well, I must say that you're just as solid there as you are everywhere else."

He laughed his delight. "You certainly know how to stroke a man's ego." But he could feel her trembling slightly as he pressed harder against her. Then he touched her in just the right place, even as she continued to arouse him, and soon she was lost. She shivered with pleasure, curling her arms around his neck and kissing him as his fingers sank inside her insistently, opening her to him. The stimulation was so acute, she almost couldn't bear it.

Their hearts raced as they came together. Valerie moaned ecstatically as Roger surged up inside her. He felt wonderful and hard, and even the intense pressure of his penetration felt exquisitely pleasurable.

"You feel great . . . so hot and tight."

"You, too," she whispered back as his sexy words drove her over the edge. She tried to settle deeper, although she was already deliciously full of him. Then he caught her about the waist and thrust upward until she gasped.

"Too much?" he asked.

"Don't stop," was all she could whimper back, her voice hoarse with rapture.

He pressed his mouth deeper into her breast. He began to move, his strokes hard and consuming, and Valerie joyously met his thrusts. The friction of their joining was wonderfully hot and abrasive, and she struggled to breathe as she hurtled swiftly toward her climax. She took his lips violently as she felt herself slipping away. Never before had she known a moment of such intense, shattering ecstasy. It seemed to last forever, yet it was over in less than a minute as Roger exploded deep inside her.

Afterward they clung to each other, both breathing hard between long, aching kisses. "You all right?" he whispered, leaning over to kiss her taut, tender nipples.

"Never better," she whispered back.

"I've never experienced anything like that in my life. I've never taken a woman so quickly—or so intensely. I just hope you didn't miss—"

"Believe me, I didn't."

He chuckled. "Actually, I was talking about foreplay."

She laughed. "I think we've been doing that for about four weeks now, Roger."

He grinned up at her, his hand stroking her bottom. "Sure you're okay, darling?"

Catching a ragged breath, she replied, "Just don't expect me to hike five miles tomorrow."

He chuckled wickedly. "Valerie, I don't know how to tell you this."

"You *do* expect me to hike five miles tomorrow?"

He shook his head. Staring into her eyes, he said, "No. I want to take you upstairs and do this all over again. But slowly this time."

"Fine," she breathed, kissing him.

VALERIE SLIPPED ON HER PANTIES before they went upstairs. But when she reached for her cutoffs, Roger took them and tossed them aside. "I told you I wouldn't let you wear those again," he teased her devilishly.

She grinned back, roving her eyes over him lovingly. He'd zipped up his jeans, but his chest was bare, his dark hair mussed. There was a heavy five-o'clock shadow along his strong jaw, a collection of whiskers that had wonderfully abraded her breasts just now. He looked very sexy.

She preceded him up the ladder, and she could feel the heat of his gaze searing her flesh....

Upstairs, lying on his mattress, they drank the wine, talked and watched the day fade through the skylight. Roger told Valerie about his apartment back in Manhattan, his house on Long Island. "I'd like to take you back there with me," he murmured, stroking her long, bare leg.

She felt warmed that he was at last hinting of their having a future together.

After a while he took their empty glasses and set them aside, a passionate gleam in his dark eyes. Without saying a word, he tugged her tank top over her head, tossing it into a far corner of the loft. He leaned over and ran his tongue over one taut nipple, then the other. She reacted with a violent moan, and he straightened to look down into her eyes. "Turn over," he whispered passionately.

Her heart lurching wildly, Valerie did as he bid, lying down on her stomach on the mattress. Roger moved aside her hair and kissed the sensitive nape of her neck. She shivered with pleasure.

"Do you know that your back is every bit as lovely as your front?" he whispered, moving his lips slowly and tormentingly down her spine. "Your skin is so soft and you taste so delicious."

Valerie bucked, but Roger merely chuckled and held her still. His feathery lips continued the torture, moving lower and lower, driving her insane. Her breathing became shallow and quick, and he noticed this with a satisfied smile. She just about came unglued as he pulled off her panties.

"You have the cutest little behind," he whispered, nipping at her playfully with his teeth. "Do you know that I've wanted to do this to you ever since I first saw you in your jeans?"

"Y-yes," she whispered back convulsively.

"Yes?" he repeated with a delighted laugh. "Why is it you women always know?"

"We just do."

Roger flicked his tongue down over her upper thigh. "You have the damn sexiest legs," he went on, even as his hand slipped beneath her to boldly stroke the nub of her passion.

Valerie could endure no more. With a mindless cry, she flipped over onto her back, pressing herself eagerly into Roger's hand, her face hot with her passionate need of him.

Above her, he was smiling with ruthless determination. "And I love your breasts," he continued, stroking the right one with his free hand.

Valerie squirmed against his touch. "They're small," she whispered.

"They're just the right size to fill my hands," he murmured. *Or suckle a baby*, he added to himself. He reeled, wondering where that shocking, provocative thought had come from. He pushed it to the back of his mind, forcing himself to concentrate on arousing her.

After a moment, with a feral cry, she pushed him onto his back and kissed him hungrily, her hands reaching for his bare chest, stroking the muscular, hairy expanse. He pulled her on top of him, settling her against his arousal. The fabric of his jeans felt rough and wonderful against her bare skin, especially as his hand gripped her bottom, guiding her into him.

"Your chest is beautiful," she half panted, studying him greedily in the fading golden light. "Do you work out?"

He nodded. "I have some exercise equipment at my apartment, and I jog several times a week."

"I thought you did," she murmured. She splayed her fingers across his chest. "I love your muscles."

He laughed wickedly. "Especially the one that's so *solid*, right?"

She wrinkled her nose at him impishly. "Especially that one."

He playfully whacked her behind, then rolled her beneath him. "Why, you little siren. I think that was a hint, lady."

"If it's not too much for you at your advanced age," she teased mischievously.

He glowered down at her. "I'm plenty young enough to wrestle down a smart-mouthed kid like you and teach you some manners."

She curled her arms around his neck. "Teach away."

He kissed her, and within seconds all levity died out and he was unzipping his jeans again. Then abruptly he rolled off her. "Just a minute, love," he said hoarsely, pulling off his jeans and briefs.

Valerie slid her eyes down Roger's beautiful naked body, studying the hair-roughened, muscular legs that she hadn't seen before now. Then her eyes fixed brazenly on his straining erection. Imagining him inside her again, so hard and deep, she felt a dizzying wave of desire. It settled in the core of her, cutting inexorably, making her ache and throb for him once more.

He settled her on top of him again. "I want to see you," he said intensely. He stared up at her, at her thick auburn hair gilded with the setting sun, at her vibrant, passion-bright eyes. Pulling her closer, he touched the place where they would be joined. "I want to see this."

His words sent her surging forward violently, taking him deeply inside her and crying out in ecstasy. She was still sensitized from their first joining, and this second coupling became even more intense and sense shattering. Pressing her hands to his shoulders, she took him hungrily, again and again, loving the sounds of his moans.

A moment later, he abruptly sat up. The motion locked them so tightly that she gasped, clinging to him and trembling.

He looked down into her eyes, blue-violet eyes that were deeply dilated, awash with tumultuous pleasure. "You okay?" he asked tenderly.

Her answer was to catch his mouth in a searing, emotional kiss. "I'm all yours, Roger," she whispered raggedly.

"Oh, Valerie. Oh, love." He rocked her there, clutching her tightly and showing her the best part of *slowly*.

IT WAS DUSK when Roger propped himself on an elbow and looked down at Valerie sleeping so peacefully beside him. He slid his eyes over every inch of her. Her face and breasts had been rubbed pink by his beard, yet she hadn't complained.

She had touched him deeply when she came to him this afternoon, and she had to have known precisely what she was doing—wearing those cutoffs again and a near-transparent tank top with no bra. Making love with her had been heavenly. This last time, he'd rocked her in his lap for a long time.

He'd managed to keep his control and had concentrated on driving her crazy. She'd become a wild woman—whimpering, clawing at his back and begging for release before he gave her what she wanted. He could still feel the scratch marks on his back where her fingernails had dug in. He considered them to be the trophies of some very delightful combat.

Their climax had been beautifully intense. Just remembering her long, slim legs wrapped so tightly about his waist, her wonderful breasts pressed against his chest, the sobbing whimpers rising in her throat, he could feel himself growing rock hard again.

At his age! He didn't know he had this in him. Oh, he knew he was capable of making love, but three times in the same night?

And there was no doubt in his mind that by morning, it would be four times—at the very least. He wanted sex with Valerie—lots of intense, passionate sex. And love... He hated to even think of how deep he was getting in there, because he knew he was already too far gone.

Yet when he looked ahead to their future, a frown drifted in. What would happen to them a few weeks from now, when they left the woods? Over the past month, they'd become such good friends, and Valerie had insinuated herself into his heart. He'd come to love having her around, and he hated the thought of losing her now.

Yet their wonderful lovemaking had not erased the essential differences that still hung between them. She was so young, and she didn't even seem to consider what she'd be losing out on by hooking up with an older guy like him. Despite the fact that she'd been hurt once before, she'd managed to hold on to her idealism and was still embracing the illusions of youth. When she reached the age where those illusions were shattered—an age he'd reached long ago—she'd surely realize how wrong they were for each other.

And while he refused to believe that Valerie was a mercenary creature, something else troubled him. How much of this attraction might be an infatuation not with him but with what he had to offer? Could the fantasy of hooking up with a famous writer, having him help launch her career, blind her to their basic differences? He already knew that she was a gifted photographer, as good as Rico, or better. She just hadn't had the right breaks yet, and those he would provide, just as he'd promised.

Yet what would happen when she achieved the success she so badly wanted and deserved? Would she still need him and want him then, or would she realize that what she'd really been after all along was not him but what he represented?

He sighed. One thing was for certain. No matter what their future brought, he had her today, and for today, he wasn't willing to give her up. Hell, he didn't know if he'd *ever* be willing to give her up.

She stirred slightly in her sleep now, instinctively moving closer to him, reaching out and touching him in just the right place. He grinned, then leaned over to kiss her sweet mouth. "Darling," he whispered, running his tongue over her lips. "Darling."

"Again?" she murmured sleepily.

But she was already curling her arms around his neck, eager to receive him.

11

THE NEXT WEEK passed blissfully for Roger and Valerie as they continued to enjoy each other and complete their work on the book. They took hikes together, made love together, shared their lives. Roger felt like a kid again as he enjoyed Valerie on every level, and she gloried in finding a man whom she could love and trust.

They made a daily sojourn to inspect the nest of the Bachman's warbler and his mate, and it was an emotionally charged moment for both the day they discovered that the nest contained a tiny white egg. They stared at the nest, embraced in the quiet sweetness of morning, watching the birds build their future together in the golden, dappled light. Neither dared to say what both were thinking—that if only things could be that uncomplicated, that simple and secure, in their own relationship, in their own future.

Privately Valerie recognized that within a short time, her sojourn with Roger here in the woods would come to an end, and that might mark the conclusion of their relationship as well. But when such unhappy thoughts flitted to mind, she'd firmly remind herself that he had not made any promises to her. Nor had she asked him for any. She had decided long ago that loving him was worth the eventual pain of parting, if it came to that.

Yet while Valerie accepted this noble resolve intellectually, emotionally it became harder and harder to face the prospect of letting Roger go, especially as the days kept trickling away and the date of their planned departure grew imminent.

Reality crashed in on them five days before they were scheduled to leave the woods. It was afternoon, and Valerie was studying a bird guide while Roger ran some errands. He seemed especially tense when he returned, joining her in the living room of the cabin.

"While I was out, the ranger gave me a message," he said awkwardly as he sat in the chair across from the couch.

"Oh?" Valerie put down her book.

"My publisher, Amory Carlisle, asked me to call him."

She stared at him in tense expectation. "And did you call him?"

He nodded, leaning toward her. "Amory wants us to meet with him and his wife in Natchez this weekend. They're coming through on their vacation, and Amory wants to check on our progress on the book."

Valerie felt the color drain from her face. "This weekend! But that's just two days away. I thought we weren't leaving here until early next week."

He sighed, drawing a hand through his hair. "Actually, Valerie, we could have left days ago."

"We could have?"

"Yes. We've got the book nailed." Staring at her with deep pride in his eyes, he added softly, "You've pulled it off, Valerie. You came through for me one hundred percent. Rico won't have to do any additional photography on the book, not that he really wanted to."

"I see," she murmured. "Well, if we've been done for days, then why didn't you—"

"I just couldn't bear . . ." He spoke hoarsely, then he turned away, his voice drifting off.

"I know," Valerie said simply. He glanced at her and they shared an anguished look.

A moment later, he cleared his throat and said, "I think we need to go on back to Natchez tomorrow."

"Tomorrow!" she cried.

"We'll both have to prepare for the meeting with Amory on Friday. I must get my notes organized, and won't you need to make prints of some of your best slides? I'm sure that Amory will want to see at least a sampling of your photography for the book."

She nodded dismally.

Roger got up and went over to join her on the couch. Taking her hand, he said seriously, "Valerie, I've been meaning to ask you something."

"Yes?" she whispered expectantly.

"If I asked you to leave Natchez with me, would you go?"

"Yes," she answered without hesitation.

"What about your dad? Wouldn't you have a problem leaving him?"

She sighed. "I'm not saying it would be easy. But Dad's known for some time that sooner or later, I might have to leave Natchez anyway, for the sake of my career."

"I see. For the sake of your career." Abruptly he got up and moved away toward the window, his back to her.

"Did I say something wrong?"

He turned to half smile at her, but there was also a sadness in his dark eyes. "Amory's going to love your work, you know."

She frowned. "Don't you think you should come over here and talk to me about this?"

He took a step closer. "I've got a better idea."

"Yes?"

"Let's go for a hike."

LET'S GO FOR A HIKE? Roger's abrupt suggestion still thoroughly perplexed Valerie as they started down the trail fifteen minutes later. Here they were, facing the most important juncture of their relationship—a time of crisis, of decision, of possible parting—and he wanted to go for a hike?

She supposed it made sense in a way. She knew from her own experience that when she was confused, anxious or frustrated, physical exercise seemed to clear her head, to make things seem simpler. Perhaps Roger wasn't trying just to avoid their problems. Hadn't he asked her to go away with him?

No, a nagging voice reminded, he'd only said, *If I asked you. . . .* That meant he hadn't *actually* asked her at all. He'd spoken no words of love, made no actual commitment to her.

But he was thinking about it. Good sign, right? And there had been an intense gleam in his eyes when he'd asked her to come out here—intense enough to make her stop off at her room to prepare herself in case he had more than exercise on his mind this afternoon.

Sighing as she brushed a strand of damp hair from her eyes, Valerie concentrated on the trail ahead of them. The May afternoon was warm and clear, the sky a bright blue. They tramped over the rolling terrain, visiting their usual haunts. Valerie took several additional shots of a magnolia warbler they'd been studying recently. And for the first time, they spotted an indigo bunting, the bird Roger had once compared Valerie's eyes to. The vivid blue bird was flitting about in the underbrush, hunting for seeds. When Valerie remarked on its striking beauty, Roger hugged her and said tenderly, "I always thought your eyes were more beautiful."

On their way back, they followed the now-familiar stream back toward the forestry tower. When they arrived at the open area where Roger had once "spotted" Valerie swimming in the nude, he paused to stare out at the water for a long moment.

She stood close by, studying him quizzically. "Why did we stop here? What are you thinking?"

He turned to smile at her. "I'm thinking that ever since I spotted you swimming here, I've dreamed of coming back here with you."

"Aha!" she said. "So that's why you brought me out here!"

He pulled her into his arms. "Are my motives that transparent, darling?"

"Yes."

She heard him groan as he tucked her head beneath his chin and stroked her hair. "It's just that ever since I spoke with Amory, all I can think of is taking you into my arms again, making love to you. . . ."

She stared up at him with awe and love. "Not that easy to face losing me, is it, Roger?"

"Oh, Valerie, no," he said, then his lips descended to devour hers.

A moment later she looked up into his eyes and asked poignantly, "What are we going to do?"

"Find a way to work it out," he replied fervently, stroking her cheek with his hand.

"Will we?"

"We will." Kissing her nose, he added thickly, "Come on. Let's go skinny-dipping."

She laughed, then glanced about warily.

"Don't worry—no one ever comes this way."

"Except for a deranged bird-watcher who likes to spot unsuspecting females from the forestry tower."

He chuckled. "But he's here with you now, darling, so you'll be safe—relatively speaking."

Valerie laughed, glancing about again. The area was open and bright, the bank softly pebbled, the cool water flowing softly, beckoning them. They'd both worked up a sweat on their hike, and the idea of frolicking in the water was very appealing. "Well, I suppose taking a dip here beats taking separate showers back at the park bathhouse," she quipped to Roger.

"Does it ever," he breathed, swooping down for another long kiss as he began unbuttoning Valerie's shirt.

It was some time before they drew apart, and when they did, there was no need to speak. Valerie smiled at Roger as she removed her clothing. He watched her finish undressing, his dark eyes solemnly devouring every inch of her flesh.

As he started pulling off his own clothes, she headed on out into the stream. The cold water felt divine against her bare skin as she waded in. She turned back to look at Roger, at the beauty of his muscular body. Even the natural surroundings seemed titillating—murmurs of wind teasing her flesh, sweet strains of bird song tickling her ears, the sensuous rhythm of the water stroking her flesh.

She moved out to where the water was waist deep, then knelt, wetting her face and even her hair. She turned to watch Roger move out to join her. For a few minutes they chased and splashed each other. Then two strong arms encircled her waist as he caught her from behind. She shuddered as his warm slippery body pressed against her back, as his hot wet mouth sank into her bare shoulder. Never before had she known a sensation like this—two hot bodies melding through the electrifying coldness of moving water! She could feel how much he wanted her as he held her tightly and moved against her thighs.

Almost violently he turned her in his arms and kissed her, his mouth cool with the taste of the stream, yet also heated with yearning. The nipples of her breasts were taut with cold and desire as she returned his possessive kiss, curling her arms about his neck and pressing her breasts eagerly against his bare hair-roughened chest.

Within seconds, he was cupping her hips to lift her onto him. Yet all at once, she was consumed with a need to prolong the sweet torment, to drive him crazy. Slipping out of his arms, she sank to her knees beneath the water, taking his maleness into her mouth and cupping him with her hand.

Even in the cool netherworld beneath the surface of the stream, she could feel the immediate, powerful effect she was having on him, especially as he surged forward, his hand tangling in her wet hair.

A moment later she came up for air.

"Valerie," he said. "Where did you learn to—er—hold your breath like that?"

She grinned up at him. "Red Cross lifesaving course."

"I'm glad you took the course," he said unsteadily. "I may shortly need to be saved."

She giggled, then swam off again playfully.

Roger started after her, but Valerie pressed low in the water, stalking him. She crouched on her knees next to him, grabbing him around his muscular thighs and repeating the provocative ritual with her mouth. She heard his distant, guttural moan as his hands sank beneath the water, gripping her face, holding her to him.

When her head broke the surface again, she saw his face outlined in full sunlight, the desire blazing in his eyes. He was breathing very, very hard. As was she. She smiled up at him, stroking him provocatively.

"Do you have any idea what you're doing?" he asked in a strangled tone. "I'm warning you, lady, you're about to be taken."

"Catch me if you can," she teased back, and swam off again.

He started after her again, but she grabbed him from beneath the water once more. This time she took him deeply in her mouth, and he almost toppled over, gripping her shoulders with desperate, trembling fingers.

Her head broke the surface and she grinned up at him "Roger, you're getting so hard, I can't wait until you're inside me."

"That does it," he said.

She frolicked off and Roger tore after her, his frustration at the boiling point. He caught up with her in the shallows near a submerged boulder, grabbing her from behind. She screamed with delight as he pulled her down with him onto the smooth rock, settling her forcefully in his lap.

"Got you!" he said with a feral growl.

"Do you ever," she panted. Indeed, he felt marvelous, nestled so deep and hard against her womb. The provocative position they found themselves in only added to the excitement both felt.

"Now you're going to get exactly what you deserve," he whispered roughly.

"Please," she begged.

He nipped at her shoulder, his breath hot on her skin as his hands reached around to knead her breasts. When he began moving inside her, the searing pressure was like nothing she'd ever felt before. Her senses were filled with the sweet scent of the stream, the earthy essence of the trees fluttering above them, and her insides, her heart and soul, were full, bursting, with him. It became so intense that she began to moan softly. He twisted her face up to his, swallowing her ecstatic whimpers with his mouth.

Her climax came with a force that made her cry out and surge forward. Roger held her fast to him. Sensing that he was still holding back a little, and wanting him to feel everything she did at that moment, she moved against him seductively. "You can let go a little, Roger. Don't worry, I can handle it."

"You're so sweet," he whispered raggedly.

Then their inarticulate cries drowned out his words as they pushed the limits and fell over the edge together. Valerie arched into Roger's climax, tilting her face to take his lips. Afterward the water at their waists barely rippled, as if unconscious of the storm of passion unleashed below.

A long time later, they walked to the bank hand in hand. Roger lay down on the pile of their clothing, pulling Valerie on top of him to shield her body from the pebbly bank. They held each other close, and there was only the sound of their labored breathing.

Then Valerie giggled.

"What?" Roger demanded.

Snuggling against him, she asked impishly, "Did I tease you unmercifully?"

He squeezed her hip. "One more little evasive maneuver on your part, lady, and I would have resorted to chains and whips."

"Roger, you're all bluster," she said.

"Just watch what happens if you push me that far again," he teased back. He cupped her chin with his hand, tilting her face so that she looked directly down into his eyes. His eyes contained a fierce, passionate warning as he said, "That little act you pulled just now—"

"Yes?" She was all breathless anticipation.

"That's a game two can play."

"Oh, I sincerely hope so, Roger," she breathed.

Staring at each other, they both became quite serious. Their breathing quickened and their hearts raced. Roger kissed her, then said huskily, "You can't know what that meant to me just now. You were so close to me, so vulnerable and giving."

Kissing him back, she said, "So were you, Roger. I've never felt like that with anyone but you." She swallowed hard, her heart thundering. Then she looked down into his eyes and whispered, "I love you."

He caught her to him fiercely. "I love you, too, darling girl."

They fell asleep in each other's arms, their senses lulled by the sweet music of the stream.

THEY AWOKE ABOUT AN HOUR LATER, dressed and went back to the cabin, having a light supper of sandwiches and fruit. Since they'd dirtied their clothes by sleeping on them on the pebbled bank, Valerie changed into her cutoffs and tank top. She wasn't just being perverse in her choice of attire, since she'd gotten rather sunburned after falling asleep on top of Roger. He made no comment about what she was wearing, but she couldn't help but delight in the heated looks he threw her way during dinner.

Valerie kept thinking of their wonderful afternoon, their incredible lovemaking at the stream. She remembered the glorious moment when she'd admitted her love to Roger, when he'd told her he loved her, too. Surely there would be a future for them now. What they had was too wonderful to be thrown away.

But they didn't talk of their future that evening. Each seemed to want, instead, simply to savor their last night together.

They spent the evening pursuing familiar pastimes. Roger screened some of Valerie's slides, while she read his latest manuscript pages. By now she'd read practically his entire book, and she had come to love the way he put words together, his excitement regarding his subject matter.

After a while, she set the pages she'd been reading in her lap and glanced up at him. He was seated across from her in a chair, the slide viewer raised to his eyes.

Clearing her throat, she said, "I believe I've detected a split infinitive."

He put down the viewer and scowled at her. "You and my editor. Just when did you become a grammarian, Valerie?"

She laughed. "I minored in journalism."

"You did? Have you done much writing yourself?"

She shrugged. "A little—for the local newspaper, that sort of thing. Actually, I only minored in journalism at the urging of my college guidance counselor. My first love is photography—definitely not writing."

"Ah, but you learned your lessons well, or you wouldn't be recognizing split infinitives." Laughing, he added, "Valerie, aren't you aware that being such a purist on grammatical matters is a bit passé?"

She stuck out her tongue at him. "Well, maybe I like being stodgy about a few things. I've never cared for split infinitives. They seem, well, sloppy."

"Sloppy?" That word brought him indignantly to his feet. He whipped off his glasses and set them down on the end table, advancing on her with a formidable gleam in his eye. "So what's my heinous split infinitive?"

She looked down at the manuscript, then quoted, "'To naturally explore.'"

"Oh, that's definitely unconscionable," he concurred gravely. His hand stroked her bare knee, and his dark eyes glittered devilishly down into hers. "So what would you prefer, my darling? 'Naturally, to explore'?" As he said the words, his hand slid up her leg.

"Hmmm," she murmured, loving the way he was touching her. "That sounds better."

His hand slid upward to her inner thigh. "'To explore naturally'?" he whispered.

"Um, better yet."

"Whatever makes you happy," he said huskily, leaning over to kiss her.

Roger sat down on the couch and pulled her into his lap. Papers went flying in every direction as he kissed her again, caressing her legs, her hips, her breasts. "I think we're going to have to go upstairs," he said. His eyes were dark, smoldering with passion as his hand slipped beneath her tank top to cup her bare breast.

"Again?" she asked with mock outrage.

"You know I can't ever get enough of you," he said thickly, burying his lips in her hair. He caught a ragged breath. "Your hair still smells like the stream. It reminds me of—"

"Okay, Roger, you've got me convinced," she said with a groan.

Seconds later she was climbing the ladder, and he was behind her. "Stop," he said.

She twisted to look down at him. "Yes?"

"Your legs," he said raggedly. "They're so incredibly lovely."

His hand slowly slid up the back of her leg, spreading gooseflesh in its wake. Grinning up at her, he insinuated his thumb beneath the frayed edge of her cutoffs, stroking her bottom as his fingers reached between her legs to stroke the sensitive flesh of her inner thigh.

"Ouch," she muttered.

"What's wrong?"

"Well, I'm a little sore—"

She could feel him stiffen, and his brows knitted in a concerned frown. "Did I hurt you today?"

"No, silly."

"Then what?"

She felt her face heating. "This is embarrassing, Roger."

"You're going to tell me—now."

"Well, you don't have to use *that* tone." As he waited, raising an intimidating eyebrow at her, she sighed explosively and said, "Actually, it was the sun."

"The sun?"

"You see, when we fell asleep near the stream, I exposed some parts I normally don't—" As he interrupted her with a ribald laugh, she added, "Roger, it's crude of you to laugh."

"Actually, I find it all rather delightful." His hand continued its wicked stroking. "So you're sunburned from sleeping buck naked with me in the woods?"

"Roger, will you kindly quit gloating?" As his fingers grew even bolder, she shivered. "So are we going upstairs or what?"

He winked at her devilishly. "I thought we'd try it on the adder."

"I doubt the ladder would stand still for that," she quipped.

He laughed, withdrawing his hand. "Go on upstairs and take off your clothes. I'll be right up."

Tossing him a bemused frown, Valerie climbed up into the loft. She lay down on Roger's bed, absorbing the smell of him from the pillow as she stared up at the stars through the skylight. She couldn't believe that after all they'd done this afternoon, she still wanted him again this badly, that she was actually trembling with expectation as she waited for him to join her.

A few seconds later, she heard him climb into the loft. Then he was staring down at her, tall, hard muscled and male. "You didn't take your clothes off," he said.

She glanced up at him unabashedly. "Maybe I want you to undress me."

He fell to his knees beside her, tossing a small plastic bottle down on the mattress. "A gentleman always obliges," he said as he unsnapped her cutoffs.

"What's that?" she asked, nodding toward the bottle.

"Just lotion. You're sunburned in some very intimate places where I'm just dying to touch you."

"Roger, you're depraved!"

"Definitely," he said, tugging off her cutoffs.

He pulled off the rest of her clothing and rolled her over, then gently rubbed the soothing lotion all over her back, bottom and upper thighs. His touch was wicked and sensual and thorough.

"Feel better now?" he asked after a while.

"Heavenly," she murmured.

He stared down at her, at the sunburned strips across her back and hips. "Hmmm . . . you must wear a pretty skimpy bikini, Valerie."

"I do," she murmured back.

He coughed. "Do you sunbathe?"

"Yes."

"Where?" he asked, his voice suddenly very tense.

She twisted to look up at him. "I sunbathe in my own backyard."

"Oh." He sounded relieved.

She lay back down, and he began rhythmically rubbing her back. "Except when I swim," she added.

"Where do you swim?" The tension was back in his voice again and the pressure of his hands on her spine was increasing.

"Oh, I have a girlfriend whose parents own a motel. When the weather's nice, Susie and I go swimming in their pool at least once a week." As his massaging hand dug into the small of her back, she added, "Hey, Roger, you're getting a little rough."

But he didn't hear her. He froze, reeling at the image of Valerie in a very skimpy bikini, her beautiful body being ogled by tourists—male tourists—as she sunbathed by a motel pool. He almost barked out, *Don't you ever, ever wear that bikini again—except for me.* Then he checked himself in time, a sudden despair washing over him. He had no right to say that to her.

As for what he wanted to do to her now . . . Abruptly he rolled her over onto her back, his slick fingers moving to the joining of her thighs. A fierce determination gleamed in his eyes.

"About this afternoon," he murmured.

She shuddered. "I thought you'd get around to that."

He slid his finger slowly downward, and she gasped and clenched against him.

He smiled, secretly pleased by her slight resistance, knowing it would make his eventual victory so much sweeter for them both. "Just relax, darling. You're going to love this."

Even as he spoke, he pressed his knees high between her thighs, prying her open to him. His finger slid inside her as his thumb stroked the nub of her passion. The sensation was so intense that she squirmed, clenching against him again.

She was tossing her head helplessly, moaning, "Roger, no . . ."

"'Roger, no'?" he repeated with a laugh. "You can say that to me after this afternoon?" He leaned over, kissing her gently. "Sorry, but it's my turn now. I told you this is a game two can play. Anyway, I love watching you like this."

She spoke convulsively. "You love—to make me lose control. But you don't."

"Ha!" he replied, moving his fingers in a particularly wicked design. "How can you say that, after what you did to me today?" Huskily he added, "I just want to drive you over the edge once, this way. I want to savor it, to look into your eyes while it happens. Don't you know that watching you feel pleasure pleases me as much as feeling it myself?"

"Roger, please . . ."

But then she was beyond speech as she began to come apart inside, clenching then releasing, again and again, until she was sure she was dying. All the time he watched her, watched her eyes grow dark and rapturous, watched her fists clench on the sheet, watched a gloss of sweat break out on her lovely face. After she went over the edge, his hand relaxed against her and he smiled.

She threw out her arms to him. "Roger."

"Not yet," he murmured. Then he leaned over and added his mouth to the conflagration between her thighs.

Valerie bucked violently, but Roger merely clamped his forearm low on her belly to hold her still. He took his time, mercilessly prolonging the torment. She reeled in the grip of a pleasure more violent and intense than she'd ever known. She felt almost as if she were connected to a hot, live current. An endless current.

When at last he moved off her, she was limp, awash in pleasure. She felt completely his in that moment, completely in love.

"Now for me," he murmured, reaching for his jeans.

But again Valerie found herself yearning for Roger to feel everything she was feeling in this stark, revealing moment. She hadn't held back, and she wasn't willing to let him do so, either. Somehow she struggled to her knees and pushed him down onto his back. "Not yet," she murmured breathlessly as she began to undress him.

He appeared intrigued and amused. "Are my words coming back to haunt me?"

"And your deeds," she added meaningfully.

By now she had his shirt off and was reaching for the lotion. He watched her with an eyebrow raised and a smile pulling at his lips.

"Just relax, Roger," she said. "You're going to love this."

He moaned his pleasure as she began rubbing the lotion on his bare chest.

"Why, Roger, I believe you have some sunburn on your shoulders," she said, giving him a look of mock reproach. "Don't worry, darling, I'll take care of it."

She continued to rub the lotion slowly, sensuously, on his shoulders and chest, trailing her fingertips suggestively down his body. His harsh breathing and deeply dilated eyes told her exactly the effect she was having on him. He tried to hook his arm around her neck to kiss her, but she pushed him away, scolding him for interfering. Then his breathing roughened even more as her fingers slipped boldly lower, unsnapping his jeans. "Let's see if you're sunburned anywhere else," she said wickedly.

Roger ground out an earthy expletive as her slick fingers touched him intimately.

She murmured, "Ah, yes. You definitely feel hot there."

That made him lurch forward, reaching for her violently. But again she was quicker. After a brief struggle, she pinned his shoulders to the mattress. "Not yet," she whispered with a triumphant grin.

"Valerie—" His eyes contained a fierce warning.

"Not yet." In her sexiest voice, she added, "I just love watching you like this."

"Oh, what did you do, tape-record everything I said earlier?"

She smiled with perverse pleasure and resumed her lovely, calculated torture. This time her lips slid slowly down his body, even as she rubbed her breasts erotically down his bare chest and stomach. By now, Roger was thrashing at the sheet. At last her lips reached just the right spot, and she delighted to his agonized moans. He whispered love words and tangled his hands roughly in her hair. After a long moment, she looked up at him, touching him seductively as she quoted, "I want to look into your eyes while it happens."

She heard his feral curse, and a split second later, she was lifted forcefully off him and he was above her, breathing hard as he wrapped her legs around his waist.

"Look into my eyes," he whispered.

She did, and saw eyes burning with passion and need, blazing down into hers. She knew in that moment that he was totally hers now, totally out of control. Then he thrust into her, and she reeled with ecstasy once more. Inside, she felt raw with sensation, every nerve ending fully exposed to him. Never had she so keenly felt the pressure and heat of him inside her. She dug her hands into his buttocks and drew him into her greedily, crying out her love.

Above her, Roger lost all control, kissing Valerie wildly and burying himself in her warm, tight sheath. Her eager surrender sent him hurtling toward a quick, violent climax.

MUCH LATER, ROGER WATCHED Valerie sleep. They lay side by side now, and he was pressed intimately into her.

"Valerie?" he whispered.

"Yes," she moaned back sleepily.

"I don't want to let you go."

"Then don't," she whispered, clutching him tightly to her.

But in the early hours of the morning, he left her.

AT DAWN, VALERIE WAS still sleeping. Roger shaved and dressed, then gathered his bird-watching gear and hiked into the woods. He went to the Bachman's warbler nest and found the female there, sitting on the egg. Any day now, the baby bird would hatch.

What was he going to do about himself and Valerie? He loved the girl so! What he'd felt with Valerie yesterday at the stream and last night had shaken him to the core. She'd been so sweet and giving. She couldn't have been more vulnerable, yet she'd been so open to him, letting him have all of her. And he'd lost control with her as he never had with a woman before.

What jarred him the most was the memory of what he'd felt both times, when he'd climaxed into her sweet, loving body. What he'd felt then had gone way beyond the desire to love, to couple. In those emotion-wrenching moments, he'd wanted what the birds had—to mate with her, to make her his forever. And he'd actually resented the birth control she was using. He'd wanted desperately to make that ultimate connection between two souls, to plant life inside her. It had even occurred to him that things would be so much simpler that way. They'd be bound together, irrevocably, from that point onward.

He couldn't be thinking of having a child—not at his age! He'd come to treasure his independence at this middle stage in life. This was no time to become encumbered with diapers and formula and a kid demanding attention at four in the morning.

But that's just what he'd wanted with Valerie. He'd wanted to love and cherish her as his wife. He'd wanted to touch her soft belly and feel it swelling with his child.

He had surely lost his mind. And she, trusting innocent that she was, had loved him unreservedly, without giving a thought to how impossible things truly were between them, without even considering all she'd have to give up for the sake of their future together.

He had to face these realities, even if she couldn't. He had to think of what was best for her, even if she refused to.

He loved her, but he just wasn't the man to make her dreams come true. And it was breaking his heart.

12

LATER THAT MORNING, Roger and Valerie were quiet as they headed back for Natchez. His car was once again crammed with all their gear.

Studying Roger sitting across from her in the driver's seat, Valerie reflected that he'd been strangely quiet all morning. They were both somewhat depressed about leaving the woods, since their time together there had been so idyllic. Valerie was more than a little concerned about how the return to civilization might affect their relationship, and she assumed that Roger was worried, too. There was the matter of her father to contend with, the fact that the two of them hailed from different geographical regions and had vastly different upbringings and outlooks—and there was the age difference that kept cropping up between them, at least from Roger's perspective.

Studying him again, she found he looked deeply immersed in thought, his handsome features tense as he stared ahead at the road. He seemed to be taking their return to Natchez even more seriously than she was. In a way, this pleased her, since it proved how important she'd become to him. But she also wondered if he didn't feel even more threatened and overwhelmed than she did regarding the stumbling blocks that they would face back in the real world. Then she thought of being with him yesterday at the stream and last night in bed, and a surge of joy filled her heart. As far as their physical relationship was concerned, there were no longer any barriers between them. They gave of themselves wholeheartedly.

And hadn't they admitted their love to each other? Surely that was the most important commitment of all. Yet still, Valerie felt worried.

Sitting across from her, Roger was immersed in many of the same fears and anxieties that she was. Their decision to return to Natchez had of necessity been so abrupt he hadn't been able to consider the full implications until now. It was one thing to decide early this morning, while away from her, that it would be best to give her up. It was something else altogether to be here with her now, steadily approaching Natchez, and to think of *actually* letting her go. Now he knew how an alcoholic must feel when he had no control over taking the next drink. She'd become his obsession—albeit a lovely one. It was becoming obvious that where she was concerned, his altruism would almost always come in a distant second to his need of her.

And right now he couldn't conceive of leaving Natchez without her. Even though he feared he was simply postponing the inevitable, he just couldn't see breaking it off yet. And besides, he rationalized, wouldn't it be better if he let some more time pass in their relationship, let her come to see how impossible it was? Let her be the one to end it?

That thought practically choked him up, especially as he glanced at her, looking so lovely beside him in her crisp white shirt and jeans, the sun glinting fiery highlights in her auburn hair as she stared at the verdant landscape. Glancing at her beautiful eyes, he again remembered the heaven of having her beneath him last night, the expression in those gorgeous blue-violet eyes when she'd lost control . . . for him.

He frowned. There was one matter that he must address, the matter of this weekend in Natchez. He'd given this a lot of thought, and they needed to get some things straight before they returned to town. Clearing his throat, he said, "I've been thinking. . . ."

She turned to smile at him. "That could be dangerous, Roger. Didn't you want to get back to Natchez before noon?"

He smiled, but inwardly groaned. How he wished they could further postpone their return—especially in the delightful manner she was alluding to—but he realized that this was impossible. "Actually, it's about this weekend."

"Yes?"

"Don't you think it would be best if we don't stay together for the next few days?"

She was taken aback. "Roger—"

He held up a hand to silence her. "Please, hear me out. We need to start thinking of your reputation. Back in Natchez, there are your father's feelings to consider, plus my publisher will be staying at my hotel." As she started to reply, he added, "Think about it a minute, darling, and I'm sure you'll agree with me."

Valerie bit her lip. She had to admit that Roger had a point, but she wasn't sure whether he was really worried about her reputation, or was just pulling away. She sighed. "Maybe you're right about our not staying together at your hotel. That might be a bit much for my dad, right off the bat. But come over to my apartment tonight and spend the evening with me, okay?"

"I just don't think that's wise, with your father around and everything."

"Roger, my parents gave me my apartment so I could have some privacy," she put in heatedly. "It's not like I'm asking you to stay the night."

"Still—"

"Still, you just care more about what everyone thinks than you care about us."

"That's not true."

"If it's not true, then kindly explain to me how your spending the evening at my apartment is any different from our staying together out in the woods."

"It's just different," he replied doggedly. "That was business."

"Oh, was it?"

He gestured in supplication. "You know what I mean."

"Unfortunately, I think I do," she replied tightly.

Roger sighed and clenched the steering wheel.

Valerie turned to stare moodily out the window. She was not at all pleased by his attitude. He seemed to be hinting that the book was the only glue that had held their relationship together.

"Valerie?" he asked after a moment.

She turned to him resentfully. "Yes?"

"Darling, please, trust me on this. We'll get it worked out in a few days' time, and then we'll be together."

"At this point, I don't see how you can talk about our having any kind of future together, if we can't even find a way to spend some time alone in Natchez." Saying the words, she turned away again.

Roger started to reply, then clamped his mouth shut. He stared grimly at the rolling terrain ahead of them; every mile they moved closer to Natchez seemed to pull him and Valerie further apart. His concern at this point was mainly for her reputation in Natchez, and he wished she could understand this.

Yet he had to admit to himself that what she had said was also partly true. He did care what her father and his publisher thought. And she had just pointed out the fallacy of his thinking, had just made him realize that the only acceptable way he could leave Natchez with Valerie was with her as his wife.

Damn, what on earth would he do?

AN HOUR LATER, there was a definite strain between Roger and Valerie as he dropped her off at her dad's house and helped her carry her things up to her apartment. Valerie was grateful that at least her father was at work. She had missed her dad, but hated the thought of injecting his presence into an already tense situation.

After she and Roger had deposited everything inside her apartment door, they faced each other awkwardly out on the stoop. "Well," he said at last, "guess I'll go get settled in at my hotel. Afterward I'll give you a call, okay? Maybe we can go out tonight."

"Don't bother trying to call me this afternoon," she replied stiffly. "I'll be down at my dad's shop making enlargements for the meeting with your publisher."

"Should I try you around five or six, then?"

"Sure. Suit yourself."

He stepped closer to kiss her then, but it was a brief, almost perfunctory kiss, and she was unyielding in his embrace.

"I'll call," were his last words to her as he went off down the stairs.

Valerie went inside and stared at her luggage and photography equipment on the floor next to her bed. She was tempted to throw herself down and sob her heart out. Despite all of Roger's reassurances to the contrary, she felt very rejected by his wanting to keep things so meticulously proper between them here in Natchez. She kept remembering all his warnings about how things would never work out between them. It seemed as though he were already distancing himself from her.

She flipped on the air conditioner, then drifted into the kitchen. She took some bread from the freezer and made herself a peanut butter and jelly sandwich. Luckily there was still one soda left in the fridge. As she ate, she began to feel a little better. She tried to see the situation more from Roger's perspective. He was older than she, and although the age difference had never mattered that much to her, she could see now that there were some differences in perspective between them, just as he had always insisted—in particular, the fact that appearances and convention would matter more to someone his age. Did the fact that he was being more conservative than she really mean that he cared for her any less?

She tried to believe he really did care, that there was hope for the two of them and their love. Right now, she had nothing else to hang on to.

VALERIE FINISHED LUNCH and unpacked, then grabbed a tray of her best slides and left her apartment. Downstairs, her car started without a hitch, and she smiled as she remembered her dad's promise to run the car at least once a week while she was gone, to keep the battery charged.

She headed toward her father's store. She hadn't informed her dad that she and Roger would be returning early, and she hoped her appearance would be a pleasant surprise for Fred Vernon.

There were no customers in the shop when Valerie walked in. Spotting her, Fred Vernon did, indeed, look delighted. He at once laid down his work and hurried around the counter. "Valerie! You're back!"

Fred hugged his daughter and kissed her forehead. "Well, this is a wonderful surprise! I wasn't expecting you until next week."

Valerie nodded. "Roger and I finished up early." She eyed Fred in his gray sport shirt and charcoal slacks, noting a healthy sheen about his complexion that she hadn't seen in a while. "You're looking great, Dad."

"And so are you," Fred replied proudly, backing off a bit. "That's a nice tan you got out there in the woods."

Valerie hoped her suntan covered her sudden blush as she recalled that she was not just tanned, but burned in some highly unmentionable places. Her blush deepened as she recalled just how she'd gotten burned in those intimate places. She coughed and said, "Well, I was outdoors a lot—photographing warblers."

"I'm aware of that," Fred said with a laugh. "That was some really excellent stuff you sent me to develop."

Valerie smiled, holding up her tray of slides. "This afternoon I'm going to make prints of some of my best shots. Roger needs them by tomorrow."

Fred frowned, adjusting his steel-rimmed glasses. "So Mr. Benedict is still in town?"

Valerie nodded, trying to sound casual as she went on, "Yes. You see, we came back early because Roger learned that his publisher is going to be in Natchez for the weekend. We're going to meet with him tomorrow."

"And after that, Mr. Benedict is heading back for New York?"

Valerie turned away to hide a sudden, pained look. She still hoped that she'd be leaving town with Roger, but she wasn't ready to discuss this with her father—certainly not in the store, where they would likely be interrupted. "Yes, I assume he will." *And I hope with all my heart that I'll be with him*, she added silently to herself.

She heard her father clear his throat. "Valerie, I—um—hope that guy didn't try anything while the two of you were out in the woods."

"Dad!" Valerie whirled, her face heated in a combination of anger and embarrassment. "This is the twentieth century, for heaven's sake. A man like Roger Benedict doesn't have to go around beating women over the head with his club and dragging them off to his cave."

"Oh, he doesn't have to, does he?" her father asked, his brow deeply furrowed.

Valerie was saved from a confrontation as a tall, lanky young man swept through the curtains at the back of the store. He was carrying an oblong cardboard box. Valerie noted that he was handsome in a boyish sort of way. He had blond hair, blue eyes and appeared to be about twenty-five or twenty-six.

At the counter, he said, "Mr. Vernon, you'll never guess what I—"

Then the young man paused in midsentence as he spotted Valerie standing next to her dad. Valerie noted that he actually blushed as he stared at her. Afterward he swallowed hard, then grinned sheepishly.

"Randy," Fred said, motioning to him, "come on over here and meet my daughter, Valerie."

Randy set the box down on the counter and eagerly swept around it.

"Valerie, meet Randy Nixon," Fred said as Randy joined them.

"I've heard all about you from your dad," Randy said eagerly as he shook the hand Valerie extended.

At Valerie's questioning glance, Fred explained, "Randy is Myrna's nephew. He just finished a six-year stint in the army, and he's at loose ends for a few weeks. So Myrna suggested he help me out here while you were gone. He's been just great with the customers."

"Oh, isn't that nice," Valerie murmured. She couldn't help but slant her dad a reproachful glance, recalling all his notes to her, all the times he'd hinted that he was having a rough time handling the shop on his own. And here, he'd had help all along! She turned to smile at Randy. "It was good of you to fill in."

"Well, it's been good for me to get some experience working with the public," Randy said. "You see, I've got a job lined up in Jackson with a new retailer. But I won't be starting until June 15, so this temporary position with Mr. Vernon has been a godsend for me."

Fred cleared his throat. "Well, Randy, what was it you discovered in the stockroom?"

He grinned again, nodding at the counter. "The missing telephoto lens to the Olympus."

"You've got to be kidding!" Fred cried. "Valerie and I have been trying to find that elusive little gadget for months now, haven't we, honey?"

"Indeed, we have," she put in. Smiling at both men, she again held up her tray of slides and said, "Well, if you two will excuse me, I have a lot of prints to make."

"Mr. Vernon showed me some of your slides," Randy told her excitedly, "and I think your work is wonderful. Look, if you need any help, well, I took some advanced photography courses in high school . . ."

"Thanks, but I think I can manage," Valerie murmured, leaving the room.

For the next several hours, Valerie tried to concentrate on the task before her as she worked in her darkroom, making enlargements from some of her best slides. She knew she couldn't complete all her work for the book this afternoon, but she could make a good start. The balance of her material could be sent in later. As she worked, she occasionally heard her father's voice drifting back to her, or Randy rummaging around in the stockroom next door. She felt badly that there was such tension between her and her dad, and she needed to talk to him about herself and Roger.

Near closing time, when the last print hung up to dry, Valerie went out to the store and took Fred aside. "Dad, why don't you and I go have a drink somewhere? I'd really like to catch up on things."

"Gee, honey, that would be delightful," Fred said. Yet he coughed, looking embarrassed. "But I'm afraid I've got other plans for the evening."

Valerie was quite taken aback. "You do?"

Fred nodded lamely. "I asked Myrna to go out to dinner with me tonight. In fact, she should be coming by here any minute."

"Oh," Valerie muttered. So she wasn't the only one who had covered some ground, romance-wise, during the past six weeks. Now she well understood why her dad looked so much in the pink.

"If only I'd known you would be back," Fred was saying awkwardly. "Look, I can cancel—"

"Oh, heavens no, don't be ridiculous," Valerie put in firmly. "Go ahead with your plans."

"Then you must come along with us, honey." Glancing toward Randy, who was at the end of the counter demonstrating a camera to a customer, Fred snapped his fingers. "Hey, why don't we ask Randy along and make it a foursome?"

"Randy?" Valerie asked, resisting an impulse to roll her eyes at her father. Randy Nixon was okay, she decided, but he seemed such an immature boy when compared with Roger that the mere thought of having dinner with him seemed absurd, that is, *if* she had even wanted to see someone else tonight, which she didn't. Smiling stiffly at her father, she said, "Thanks, Dad, but I'll have to take a rain check. You see, I'm not free for the entire evening, just for an hour or so."

Fred was scowling at this news when abruptly Myrna Floyd burst into the shop, looking pretty as a summer flower in a pink shirtwaist dress. "Valerie!"

Valerie rushed over to hug her friend. Myrna then asked a dozen questions about Valerie's experiences out in the woods, and the next few minutes passed quickly as Valerie filled Myrna and Fred in on some of her activities with Roger. Of course she left out the entire matter of their romance, making the adventure out in the woods sound very innocent and professionally focused. Myrna delighted in everything Valerie said, while Fred's expression was more guarded. However, through it all, Valerie did not miss the occasional secretive glances Myrna and Fred exchanged. Indeed, a lot had been going on in her absence, she realized.

Myrna, too, insisted that Valerie and Randy should join them for dinner, but Valerie demurred, explaining again that she wasn't free for the entire evening. Taking her cue, Randy told his aunt that he really had to do his laundry tonight, and urged the others to go on while he locked up. Valerie tossed Randy a grateful glance as she left.

Waving goodbye to her father and Myrna, Valerie got into her car and headed home. She felt relieved that she didn't have to spend the evening being falsely cheerful in the company of her dad, Myrna and Randy.

While she was glad that Myrna and her dad had evidently found each other during her absence, she also couldn't contain a small stab of resentment and jealousy. She was used to her dad always being there for her. And, of course, she had really worried about leaving him alone for six weeks—foolishly so, it would seem. Here it was, her first night back, and he didn't need her around. He wasn't even free to have a drink with her.

She'd been worried about a problem that didn't exist! Of course she couldn't blame her dad. She knew he had every right to seek his own happiness. Yet this new little twist, plus her troubles with Roger, put Valerie in a mood to feel very sorry for herself.

She walked into her apartment to a ringing telephone. "Where have you been?" Roger barked as soon as she answered.

Valerie smiled as she sat down on her bed with the receiver at her ear. "Hi, Roger." They'd only been apart a few hours, yet she realized now how much she'd missed him—even his barking.

"You're not going to get out of this with sweet talk," he said firmly. "I've been trying to get you for over an hour."

"I was making the prints for our meeting tomorrow, remember? Then I helped my dad close up shop. Myrna came in and we all got to gabbing. Okay, Sherlock?"

"Oh." Sounding somewhat mollified, he added, "Everything okay with your dad?"

"He's fine."

"Well, I'm glad you got the prints ready. You see, Amory and his wife have already arrived here at the hotel. I set up our meeting for noon tomorrow at the hotel coffee shop. Okay with you?"

"Fine."

"I was wondering if you'd have dinner with me," he continued.

"I thought you'd never ask," Valerie said happily. In her sexiest croon, she added, "Why don't you come on over here, fella, and I'll—um—feed you."

She heard him groan. "You know how I feel about that. We need to be careful about—"

"Don't worry," she answered, her voice edged with resentment. "My dad took Myrna Floyd out to dinner, so my sacred reputation—and especially yours—will be safe."

She heard him sigh explosively. "Why can't you see my side in this?" Before she could answer, he went on, "No, let's not start up. Look, will you go out with me? I'm kind of pressed for time, because I promised Amory I'll meet him later for a drink here at the hotel."

"And you wouldn't want to be seen there with me—especially not at night."

"Valerie, will you give me a break?"

But Valerie was feeling very hurt by his stubborn refusal to spend time alone with her here in Natchez. "Look, Roger, if you don't care enough to come over here, why don't you just forget it?"

He whistled. "I'm beginning to feel like a sex object."

"I didn't hear one complaint on that score while we were out in the woods," she pointed out heatedly.

"That was a different situation, as you know. You're very aware of my feelings about how we conduct ourselves here in town. I'm doing this for you, for heaven's sake. I'm willing to live with some temporary frustration, and I don't see why you can't make the sacrifice, too."

"I would—if you'd offer me a valid reason. And you haven't."

He was silent for a long moment. At last he said, "Obviously, we're getting nowhere with this."

"I quite agree," she rejoined. "I should have gone out to dinner with my father, Myrna and Randy."

There was a moment of tense silence, then Roger asked roughly, "Who's Randy?"

"My father's new clerk."

"Don't move," he snapped, and hung up.

Valerie frowned at the receiver a moment, then smiled, wondering how long it would take Roger to get over here.

It took him twenty minutes, and his expected knock at her door was sharply insistent. She opened the door and he entered, striding over to her dining area and tossing a pizza box down on the table. Turning to her, he asked, "Valerie, why do you have to be such a child sometimes?"

"A child?" she repeated furiously. "It seems to me that you're the one putting up barriers. And that seems pretty childish to me."

"I'm the only one facing reality." He began to pace, shaking his head. "I gave perfectly valid reasons why we should be more careful here in Natchez, and then you..." He paused, catching a ragged breath and staring at her starkly.

"Yes, Roger?"

His gaze roved over her intimately, in anguish and hunger. "You know, on the way over here, I had a hundred things planned to say to you."

She stepped closer to him and could literally feel the tension radiating between them as she stared boldly into his dark, passionate eyes. "And now?"

"Now I'm not in a mood to talk."

Roger pulled her into his arms. He kissed her fiercely and his hand tugged impatiently at the buttons of her shirt. A second later, he was kneading her breasts through her lacy bra, and both of them were struggling to breathe. His hands slid to her waist, and he began unzipping her jeans.

"Why can't I ever get enough of you?" he asked hoarsely, pulling her to the bed.

They fell across the bed together, their limbs entangled and their mouths deeply locked. Roger undid her bra as she pulled at his shirt buttons. He kissed her neck and breasts, and she slid her hands provocatively down his chest and stomach. Soon she was unbuckling his trousers, and he was tugging at her panties.

"Did you . . . ?" he asked, his eyes glazed and fervid above her.

"Yes," she replied breathlessly. "I had a feeling we'd end up this way tonight."

"Don't we always?" he asked poignantly.

Her heart pounded as she heard her jeans hit the floor. He moved away from her for a moment, shucking the rest of his clothing. Then he sat up against the headboard and whispered, "Darling, come here." The burning hunger in his eyes made her tremble as he pulled her into his lap. She took him eagerly inside her, staring down at him feverishly and breathing in ragged gasps.

"I wanted you and you hurt me when you pulled away," she said achingly.

"I didn't pull away," he said.

"Yes, you did."

"I didn't." He thrust up high and she collapsed against him, clinging to him as they kissed each other hungrily. A moment later his mouth moved to her breast, his teeth cutting with pleasurable sharpness. Valerie lost control, her hips moving in a frenzy of need that drove Roger crazy. She plunged her tongue into his ear and whispered earthy messages of love and need. He responded wildly, his mouth seeking hers roughly as his thrusts deepened.

At last she panted, "Please, I want you to—"

"I know," he said. Then he caught her about the waist and climaxed with an intensity that tore a cry of pleasure from them both.

Afterward, lying in his arms, Valerie felt tender, loved, all over. She reveled in the feeling, knowing how much Roger had needed her.

"Hell, the meeting with Amory," he said much later.

She watched him dress by the light of a lamp. Then he walked over to the table and picked up the box holding the now-cold pizza. "In the oven or in the refrigerator?" he asked her.

"In the refrigerator," she replied. "I'm not hungry anymore."

He chuckled and placed the box in the refrigerator. Then he returned to the bed, glancing unabashedly at her lovely nakedness. He leaned over and nuzzled her stomach, then kissed each taut, tender nipple. "Behave yourself," he scolded as he drew the sheet over her.

She smiled at him as he left. But after he was gone, her depression returned. So they loved each other wildly and desperately. Did that really solve anything?

13

VALERIE AWAKENED the next morning feeling more hopeful than she had felt the previous night. The bright warm day helped to elevate her mood. She kept reminding herself that Roger *had* come to her last night, despite his resolve that they should keep things very proper between them now that they were back in Natchez. Surely he wouldn't be able to leave town without her.

She had dressed and was lamenting the fact that there was nothing in her apartment to eat except cold pizza when her father knocked on her door and invited her downstairs to have breakfast with him. She happily consented, and they both dived into the delicious meal of sausages and pancakes that Fred had prepared.

"Well, did you and Myrna have a good time last night?" she asked him over coffee in the dining room.

Fred set down his cup and spoke earnestly. "I really like Myrna, Valerie."

"Hmmm, I've noticed. This is beginning to sound serious, Dad."

"I suppose it is," Fred admitted. "You see, I can really talk to Myrna—even about your mother. We both loved Mary, so we have a lot to share there."

"I know you do," Valerie murmured. "And I'm so glad you have someone you can open up with. We all need that."

"We haven't made any definite plans yet, of course," Fred put in quickly. "But we are going to be spending a lot more time together."

"Good," Valerie said. Encouraged by his confiding in her, she added, "Dad, there's something I need to tell you, too."

Fred's expression grew guarded. "Yes?"

Valerie drew a deep breath, then blurted, "It's very possible that I'll be leaving Natchez with Roger Benedict next week."

"What?" Fred exclaimed, frowning fiercely. "You mean you're going to marry that man?"

"Not exactly," Valerie answered honestly. "But we're in love."

"You're in love?" Fred repeated with a disbelieving laugh, tossing down his napkin. "Then I suppose that gives you the perfect excuse to simply ignore reality."

"What reality, Dad?" Valerie asked patiently.

"That man is way too old for you. My God, Valerie, I never thought I'd see the day when you would consent to become the mistress of a man like that."

"Roger is a fine man," Valerie put in heatedly. "And I don't at all appreciate your trying to cheapen what we have. The two of us are in love, and we simply want to pursue this and see where it leads just like you and Myrna."

Fred laughed bitterly. "I'm afraid I see some differences, my dear. I'd never expect Myrna to live with me without the benefit of marriage. But I suppose that's the excuse a nineties man like Benedict uses to avoid making a commitment to a woman."

"For heaven's sake, Dad! Roger just wants to be sure. His first marriage didn't work out—"

"So he's divorced, too?"

"I can see that there's no reason to even discuss this with you," Valerie said through gritted teeth. "You have a closed mind about Roger. And besides, you just don't want me to leave Natchez."

"That, too," Fred admitted.

The two were glowering at each other when the front doorbell rang. Fred excused himself to answer the door, and a moment later, Valerie walked into the living room as Fred was ushering in Myrna.

Myrna, who hadn't spotted Valerie, was frowning at the furniture and saying, "Fred, I'm sure I left the keys to my shop here last night. I believe I pulled them out of my pocket right after I took off my shoes.... Aha! There they are on the end table."

Valerie glanced at her dad and noted with perverse satisfaction that he looked embarrassed. In the meantime Myrna, with her key ring now in hand, had spotted Valerie. "Well, good morning, honey," she said with a bright smile. "How good it is to see you here with your dad."

Valerie smiled at her friend. "Dad invited me down for breakfast." Then she glanced back at Fred and sighed as she saw the look of reproach again flashing in his eyes.

The telling look that passed between father and daughter was not lost on Myrna. "Well," she said, clearing her throat, "guess I'd best get on down to my shop before the customers start beating down the door."

After Fred saw Myrna out, a tense silence settled between father and daughter. Then Fred said, "Valerie, about what just happened... Look, Myrna and I were only watching TV last night, and she left her keys—"

"Dad, what you and Myrna do is your business," Valerie cut in stiffly. Pointedly she added, "I do recognize the fact that both of you are adults." She glanced at her watch and sighed. "Thanks for the breakfast. For now, I've an important meeting to prepare for. So, if you'll excuse me..."

Fred frowned as he watched his daughter turn and walk out the front door.

THE MEETING WITH ROGER'S publisher and his wife was scheduled for noon in the coffee shop of the downtown hotel where Roger and the Carlisles were staying. Roger and the couple were already at their table when Valerie arrived. The two men stood as Valerie approached. She wore a light-weight summer suit, and her hair was upswept. Her portfolio was tucked beneath her arm.

Valerie smiled and murmured pleasantries as Roger introduced her to Amory Carlisle and his wife, Elaine. While the couple was very friendly, Valerie noted at once that Roger's manner today was stiffly formal, and he looked preoccupied. But she didn't really have time to consider what might be troubling him as she turned her attention to the Carlisles.

Amory was tall, slender and looked to be in his late forties, with a balding head and a perpetual smile. Elaine appeared to be a bit younger—she was very pretty, stylishly dressed and a little on the plump side. Her manner was down-to-earth and friendly, and Valerie warmed to her at once.

At first they ordered and made small talk. The Carlisles had arrived in town yesterday afternoon, and Elaine had already fallen in love with Natchez. "You must adore living here," she told Valerie breathlessly. "Amory and I saw Dunleith and Melrose this morning, and we were simply blown away. I can't wait for us to continue touring homes this afternoon."

"Elaine is already convinced that we should do a book on Natchez," Amory confided to Valerie. "I tried to convince her that there are already a number of good ones out." Throwing Elaine an admonishing glance, he added, "I should know. I bought most of them this morning."

The four of them laughed as the waiter brought their salads. "I wish we could stay here an extra week," Elaine was saying. Glancing at Amory fondly, she added, "But we don't want to be late for Susie's big event, now do we, dear?"

Amory chuckled. "My dear, our daughter's baby is not due for another four weeks."

"Well, one never knows," Elaine replied to her husband. "It is Susie's and Steve's first child."

As Valerie glanced confusedly from Elaine to Amory, Roger explained, "Amory and Elaine are expecting their first grandchild shortly. They were telling me all about it right before you arrived."

Valerie was taken aback by Roger's words, for he had made the announcement unsmiling, without a hint of warmth. What was wrong with him today? she wondered. She quickly recovered and turned, smiling, to the Carlisles. "Well, congratulations to you both."

"Tell me that after I arrive at the poorhouse," Amory replied ruefully. "Before we left New York, Elaine had the nursery at Steve and Susie's apartment so crammed with baby things that they couldn't get in the door. Now, Grandma here is buying out Natchez, as well."

Elaine waved him off. "Oh, Amory. You're exaggerating, as usual. Just because I wanted to buy the child a few necessities—"

"A few necessities?" Amory repeated with a laugh. "Ah, yes. What child can live without nineteen stuffed animals, three walkers and two strollers? Not to mention an old-fashioned mammy rocker."

"Amory and I found that at an antique store this morning," Elaine confided eagerly to Valerie. "I just couldn't resist it. You see, the mother can rock and do her sewing, while the baby sleeps in a built-in cradle next to her. I always say that old-fashioned ideas are quite often the best. Susie will adore the rocker, I know."

"If I can ever get the contraption shipped back to New York," Amory put in with a groan.

Valerie laughed as she continued to listen to the Carlisles excitedly discussing their coming grandchild. Yet through it all, Roger was grimly silent, and Valerie was becoming more and more perplexed at his withdrawal.

Once they'd finished their meal, Amory at last got down to business. "Well, Valerie, I hope I don't seem unnecessarily nosy in wanting to check on yours and Roger's progress on the book."

"Not at all," she was quick to assure him.

"The fact of the matter is, I was very concerned after I learned that Rico Romero was injured. You see, we're going to be on a very tight production schedule with this book, and our promotional campaign is already planned. A delay at this point—"

"Please, I understand completely," Valerie put in.

"Good," Amory said with a smile. "Roger and I met last night and went over most of his notes. Looks like the text for the book is in great shape. Just a matter of getting it typed."

"And now you'd like to see my photographs, right?" Valerie asked.

"Well, if you don't mind," Amory said kindly.

"Of course not," she replied, handing him her portfolio.

For several long minutes, there was a dead silence as Amory glanced over the color photographs. Valerie tried to catch Roger's eye, without success. He looked downright unreachable as he stirred his coffee and occasionally glanced at Amory.

At last Amory looked up, shaking his head. "My, my," he said slowly. Turning to his wife, he added, "Elaine, you must see these. They're magnificent."

For the next ten minutes, Amory and Elaine ranted and raved over Valerie's photography. Amory was practically beside himself, jubilant that production on the book would not have to be delayed. Roger was tensely silent throughout the exchange, except at one point, when Elaine turned to him and said, "Roger, isn't Valerie marvelous?"

Roger glanced at Valerie, then smiled. "She is that," he said quietly to Elaine.

After they'd exhausted the subject of the bird book, Amory grilled Valerie on her background—her education, the other types of photography she had done. Then he said excitedly, "You know, Valerie, we've been wanting to do a big, glitzy book on the south of France. Would you be interested in doing the photography for us?"

Valerie was floored. "Are you kidding, Mr. Carlisle?"

"Please, it's Amory. And I'm not kidding at all."

Valerie glanced at Roger expectantly, but found no encouragement in his expression. Nevertheless, she turned back to Amory and said, "I'd be delighted to do the photography for you."

Amory grinned at her words. But he had also evidently picked up on the tension between Valerie and Roger. He turned to Roger and added apologetically, "And I'm hoping you'll want to take on this project, too, Roger. Your other travel books have done so well for us, so of course we'd want you to write the text."

"Bully for you," Roger said dryly.

Amory looked taken aback a moment, then brightened. "Well, you two. Do you think we can work out a deal?"

"I'm sure Valerie will be happy to oblige you," Roger said stiffly, "but as for me, Amory, I must regretfully decline. My foreseeable future involves other activities."

Valerie glanced at Roger, stunned. What on earth was his problem today? Here, Amory was handing them on a silver platter the perfect solution to their relationship, an opportunity for them to spend more time together while they did another book. And Roger was turning this down?

There could be only one reason for his acting this way. He was telling her very bluntly—and very publicly—that he wanted her out of his life.

Valerie felt devastated and betrayed. It was all she could do not to break down in front of everyone. Somehow she managed to keep making small talk with Amory and Elaine as the four ate their dessert and drank another cup of coffee. Afterward Elaine said brightly, "Well, Roger, won't you and Valerie come sight-seeing with us this afternoon?" To Valerie, she added, "It would be a real privilege to have a native along."

Not giving Roger a chance to reply, Valerie said, "Thanks very much for the invitation, Elaine, but I'm afraid I promised my dad I'd help him out at his shop this afternoon." After uttering the white lie, she glanced at her watch. "In fact, I'm late now."

Amory and Elaine murmured their regrets that Valerie couldn't join them, and she thanked them for the meal and prepared to leave. "May I count on you for the new book, Valerie?" Amory asked as they shook hands.

Valerie glanced at Roger and still found only a blank wall staring back at her. Tilting her chin slightly, she replied evenly to Amory, "Yes, you can count on me."

"I'll be in touch, then," Amory said.

Valerie smiled at him, said, "Thanks again," and left the restaurant without looking back.

AFTER VALERIE LEFT, Amory glanced perplexedly at Roger. "Is something troubling you?"

"No, not at all," he replied tersely.

"You really don't want to do another book with Valerie?"

"Frankly, no."

"But she's wonderfully talented."

Roger raised an eyebrow as he sipped his coffee. "So you've eminently noticed."

Amory and Elaine exchanged a bemused glance, then Amory laughed and said, "Don't tell me that you've fallen for that lovely young thing? Not a relic like you."

Roger turned his formidable scowl on Amory. "I'll have you know, Carlisle, that I'm a man in my prime—hardly a relic."

Amory laughed. "You have fallen for her! I've never seen you get this hot under the collar over anything, Benedict."

"Oh, hush, Amory," Elaine put in. "I think it's lovely." Turning to Roger, she added, "Just think, a May-December romance!"

Roger glowered at them both.

OUTSIDE THE RESTAURANT, Valerie was trembling with hurt and anger as she arrived at her car. She still couldn't believe that Roger had done this to her, betraying her and rejecting her in front of Amory and Elaine. She was tempted to go home and cry her eyes out. But then she decided no, she'd wait for Roger here, confront him and get it over with.

A few moments later, she spotted him leaving the hotel. She met him toward the front of the parking lot. "Roger, will you kindly explain to me what all of that was about?" she asked angrily. "If you're competing for jerk of the year, I can tell you now that there's no contest!"

He sighed, and there was a deep sadness in his brown eyes. "Valerie, I'm sorry. But I told you things would never work out between us. Today just drove it all home for me, especially as I sat there listening to Amory and Elaine." He continued passionately, "They're my best friends. I've known them all my life. Do you realize that Elaine Carlisle is a year younger than me? And already she and Amory are expecting their first grandchild."

"So? What does any of that have to do with you and me?"

"I'm afraid it has a great deal to do with the two of us, my dear," he said with deep regret.

"You just care more about what your friends think than you care about me," she accused.

"I do care about you, Valerie. But now I know that we've been living in a fantasy world. What we had out in the forest was wonderful. But here in the real world, we just don't have a basis for building a lasting relationship. I can't give you the things you're looking for at this stage in your life."

"It's the damn age difference again, isn't it?"

He swallowed hard. "I've tried to tell you repeatedly that it's not just the age gap between us, but the differences in perspective that it represents."

"Our perspectives seemed pretty compatible last night."

He groaned, running his hand through his hair. "Valerie, what we've had in bed has been fantastic. I'll never forget—"

"We've had a great deal more than that and you know it. We enjoyed many activities together out in the woods."

"That's true," he conceded, taking a step closer and offering her a resigned smile. "I was your teacher, and you were my protégé. But the meeting today drove home for me the fact that that's over, too." Poignantly he added, "You're well on your way now, darling, just as you should be. Amory's response to your work more than demonstrated that to me. You have a very bright future ahead of you."

"Why can't that future include you?" she asked with frustration and despair.

He sighed again, giving her an openhanded gesture. "Don't you see? I've taught you everything I can now. And you've obviously gotten everything you need from me."

"Are you intimating that I was only along for what I could get from you?" she asked furiously, wounded by his last words. "Damn, I can't believe your arrogance! Then maybe you just used me, too, huh, Roger? It was fun while it lasted, but now it's over, right?"

He shook his head wearily, then glanced at his watch. "I'm sorry, Valerie. Look, I've got to go. For some reason, Rico is still in town. He left a message for me here at the hotel, and promised him I'd go fishing with him this afternoon."

"Fine," Valerie said tersely. "Don't let me keep you."

He reached out to touch her arm. "I'll give you a call later."

She pulled away. "Don't bother."

They exchanged a hot, anguished look, then Valerie turned on her heel and walked away.

14

VALERIE TRIED TO RESTRAIN her tears as she drove home. So it was really over between her and Roger.

Intellectually Valerie tried to tell herself that she had no real reason to be angry and bitter. Roger had never made any promises to her. And hadn't he warned her from the beginning that he didn't feel they could build a lasting relationship? She should be grateful for the time they'd shared together.

Yet even as she tried to embrace this noble resolve, emotionally she was ready to strangle him. He'd broken up with her because he'd discovered that his friends were expecting their first grandchild? It seemed the lamest of excuses. Surely this was just his weak rationale to cover the fact that he didn't care enough about her to make a commitment to their relationship.

Valerie had made it home to her apartment and was just about to have a good cry, when a rap sounded at her door. Desperately hoping the caller was Roger, she flung open the door, only to find Myrna standing on her stoop. Her shoulders drooped. "Oh, hi, Myrna."

Looking preoccupied, Myrna asked, "May I come in for a minute?"

"Sure," Valerie said, admitting her then closing the door.

"I can't stay long. You know how agitated Sadie gets when I ask her to handle the shop by herself for long periods."

Valerie forced a smile as she gestured at her rattan love seat. "What's on your mind?"

Myrna plopped herself down on the love seat, and Valerie sat down in a chair across from her. "I hope you didn't get the wrong impression when I dropped by this morning."

"Oh, you mean when you came by for your keys? Don't give it another thought."

"It was just a reflex action—I mean, my leaving the keys. After Fred and I went out to dinner last night, he invited me here to watch a movie on TV. And you see when I take off my shoes, I always remove the keys from my pocket."

Valerie held up a hand. "Look, Myrna, you don't have to explain anything to me. Like I told Dad this morning, what the two of you do is your business."

"But it matters very much to Fred and me what you think— I mean, what your feelings are about—"

"Myrna, I'm very glad that you and my father have found each other," Valerie replied with all the sincerity she could muster. And, saying the words, she burst into tears.

"Oh, my!" Myrna cried, looking crestfallen. "Oh, dear! I just knew this was upsetting you!"

Valerie wanted to deny her friend's words, but by now, she was sobbing uncontrollably. Myrna fetched Valerie a box of tissues and a glass of water, then hovered nearby, fretting and patting Valerie's shoulders until she began to calm down. When the sobs subsided into whimpers, Myrna insisted Valerie join her on the love seat. Myrna hugged her and said, "Valerie, I'm so sorry."

"I'm the one who should apologize," Valerie replied, wiping her eyes. "I was just about to have a good cry when you arrived."

"Oh, no," Myrna cried. "Are you that upset that your father is seeing me? Because if you are—"

"Don't be ridiculous," Valerie said with a laugh that was half a sob. "It's not because of you and dad at all. It's because of Roger and me."

"Aha!" Myrna said, nodding as her eyes widened. "Fred was really worried about you being alone with Mr. Benedict out in the woods. Did something happen?"

"Did it ever!"

Myrna frowned fiercely. "Tell me what the scoundrel did."

Valerie laughed again. "He's not a scoundrel. Not at all."

"Then what on earth happened?"

Valerie expelled a ragged sigh, then said, "We fell in love."

"Oh, Valerie! I think that's wonderful. But is that a reason to fall apart, dear?"

"It is if the one you love doesn't want you."

"Oh, dear. Bless your heart. Want to tell me about it?"

Valerie nodded, then spilled out to Myrna the entire story of her failed romance with Roger. She told Myrna everything that happened during the luncheon with the Carlisles and afterward. "I should have known," she concluded ruefully. "Roger kept warning me that things would never work out between us. He's twenty years older than me, and he kept insisting that we want different things from life—although I never really understood this."

"Perhaps you'll understand better when you're twenty years older," Myrna put in wisely.

"Are you taking his side now?" Valerie asked indignantly.

"No. I'm just saying that at my age, maybe I can understand a little better what Mr. Benedict means. And maybe you will when you're older."

Valerie sighed. "I guess things wouldn't have worked out between us, anyway. Dad heartily disapproved of Roger."

"Don't think of what your father wants," Myrna advised. "Think of what you want."

"I want Roger, but he doesn't want me! He just used me to have a fling and to finish up his book. And he even had the gall to accuse me of using him. He said that now I've gotten everything I want from him."

Myrna squeezed Valerie's hand. "Now, honey, that's just your hurt and confusion talking—and his, too. From everything you've told me, I'm sure your Mr. Benedict is very much in love with you. But that man is twenty years older than you. He feels he can't ask you to give up your future for him."

"Well, if he thinks that, he's wrong."

"Then you're going to have to go to him and tell him that, honey."

"And have him shove me away again?" Valerie asked bitterly. "I think my pride has been dragged through the mud enough for one day."

"Then you're going to have to decide what matters to you more—Roger, or your silly pride."

"Myrna, you *are* on his side!"

"No, honey, I'm on your side. And I think he is, too."

Valerie sniffed, wiping her tears. "I beg your pardon?"

"From what you've told me of his behavior, I'm sure he thinks he's doing what's best for you."

Valerie frowned. "I hadn't thought of it quite that way before."

"Well, start thinking of it that way. If you want him, you're going to have to go after him."

Valerie thought over Myrna's words for a long moment, then nodded. "You know, I think you're right."

"And don't worry about your father," Myrna added wisely. "I'll take care of Fred. All he really wants is for you to be happy."

After Myrna left, Valerie felt incredibly calm. Myrna had really helped her to see things more from Roger's perspective. Of course it was entirely possible that he had broken up with her for her own good, and she was the only one who could set him straight.

She couldn't wait to talk to him again. But unfortunately, he'd gone fishing with Rico and probably wouldn't be back for several hours. She picked up the phone and called Amory

Carlisle at his hotel. Luckily she caught him before he and Elaine left for their afternoon sight-seeing. "I'm sorry, Amory," she told him, "but I have to turn down the assignment for the book set in France. I have a different priority right now. . . ."

WHILE VALERIE WAS TALKING with Amory Carlisle, Roger was fishing with Rico at a small landing on the Mississippi south of Natchez. The day was sunny and bright, and the sun gleamed on the broad waterway as a barge drifted slowly past. Rico and Roger sat in folding chairs at the edge of the water, watching their lines.

While they hadn't had much luck fishing, Roger had caught up on things with Rico. He'd been relieved to observe that Rico's cast was gone now and that he was getting around quite well.

Ever since Roger had returned to Natchez and had received Rico's message, he'd wondered why his friend still hadn't returned to New York. This afternoon was providing the answer, as Rico spoke endlessly of Chloe Gerard, the young Cajun girl Roger had hired as his nurse. Roger realized that Rico, the avowed playboy, had at last fallen deeply in love. All he could talk about was how beautiful Chloe was, how lovely her laughter, how sweet her temperament. . . .

"Except when she gets mad," Rico now added with a grin. "Wow, does that girl have a Cajun temper."

"And just what have you done to provoke her?" Roger asked.

The grin broadened. "Well, I've been chasing her around on crutches for six weeks now, but no dice. Chloe, she's a half-pint, but she's really strong, man. She must have wrestled alligators back in Louisiana."

Roger laughed. "Well, she must have quite a lot of charm for you to stick around for six weeks without—er—having your wicked way with her."

Rico drew himself up irately. "Hey, just what kind of girl do you think Chloe is? She's only twenty, for heaven's sake, and she's had a very sheltered upbringing. She says we have to get married first."

"And?" Roger literally could not believe his ears.

Rico spoke defensively. "I can understand her feelings— especially at her age."

"You don't mean to tell me you actually want to marry this girl, without—er—"

"Hell, yes," Rico said.

Roger whistled. "My, my, you must have really fallen for her hard, if this girl has managed to totally realign your values." And wasn't he quite aware of that process himself?

"I'm just worried about taking her away from Natchez," Rico continued with a frown. "She's quite devoted to her family."

Roger waved him off irritably, as his thoughts turned unhappily to his own situation with Valerie. "Just marry the girl, Rico. It's not like you have *real* problems."

Rico frowned at Roger. "Hey, what's eating you today, man?"

Roger sighed. "It's Valerie."

"Aha!" Rico said with a laugh. "I knew you had fallen for her. You were such a grouch that day we all had lunch together. If looks could have killed, I would have been jambalaya." When Roger merely glowered at him, he added, "So you pursued a little more than the birds out in the woods?"

"It was mutual," Roger replied stiffly.

"Ah, yes. I could have told you that, too. So, if you and Valerie have a thing now, why aren't you with her this afternoon, instead of fishing with me?"

Roger clenched his jaw. "I broke up with her two hours ago."

Rico whistled. "You've got to be kidding! Did she throw you over for someone else?"

"Of course not," Roger barked. "I just decided that breaking it off would be best for her."

Rico rolled his eyes. "That's a new one."

"Rico, I'm twenty years older than she is. I can't give her the things a girl her age wants."

"Such as?"

"Well, children."

Rico grinned and shook his head. "You know, Roger, you really can be a prig sometimes. My old man waited exactly two years after my mom died before he remarried a girl half his age. Now he's fifty-two years old, with a new baby on the way, and he's tickled pink. I say, more power to him. I know my mom wouldn't have wanted him to waste away mourning her. She would have wanted him to seek his own happiness."

"I'm glad he has, but what's the point?" Roger asked.

"The point is, what's wrong with marrying a girl half your age?"

Roger sighed, staring out at the river. "It's not the solution for everyone, I'm afraid."

Rico elbowed Roger. "You're just afraid you're getting too old to keep her in line, huh, man?"

"Not at all," Roger replied forthrightly, although Rico had just touched on one of his fears—especially after last night.

Rico sighed dramatically. "Poor Valerie. She must really be torn up about this. Hey, why don't I take her out to dinner tonight and see if I can cheer her up? I'll report back to you on everything, of course. Wouldn't you prefer to go back to New York knowing she's doing better?"

Roger glowered at Rico. His friend's words suddenly and forcefully reminded him that if he gave up Valerie now, other men would ask her out, touch her, take her to bed . . . Rico, Randy, whoever. They'd all want her, of course.

Suddenly every male instinct in Roger screamed out, *No way*.

Roger realized that everything was wrong. He'd gotten scared and broken things off with Valerie too quickly. He'd behaved like an ass. There was no way around it. What he and Valerie really needed was more time, time to give their love a chance, time to work things out.

Hell, who was he kidding? He didn't just want more time with her, he wanted it all! As long as he lived, he would never let her go again, never let another man have her. She was *his*, by God. His . . .

"Well, man, should I give Valerie a call?" Rico was prodding.

Throwing the younger man his steeliest glare, Roger replied, "You do that and I'll break both your legs."

Rico whistled, looking properly chastised as he held up a hand. "Hey, man, no problem. I was only trying to be helpful. You don't have to get violent about it."

Roger stood. "I think it's time for us to return to Natchez."

"Sure, man, whatever you say."

Rico tried his best to conceal a satisfied grin as the two men gathered up their gear.

15

BY THE TIME ROGER RETURNED to his hotel, got cleaned up and changed, it was after five o'clock. He was rushing through the lobby, intent on leaving for Valerie's house, when he ran into Amory Carlisle.

"Hey, Roger!" Amory called out.

Roger paused, struggling to contain his impatience as Amory walked up to join him. "Amory, I'm sorry, but I'm really in something of a hurry."

"Looking for Valerie?" Amory asked with a grin.

"How did you guess?"

"Well, she was here about an hour ago, looking for you."

"She was?"

"Yes." Amory frowned. "She also called earlier to turn down the assignment on the book set in France. She told me she has a different priority right now. Any idea what that might be, Benedict?"

"Look, Amory," Roger said, running his hand through his hair, "Can you leave the book on hold for Valerie and me? I'll explain everything later. But for now, I've got to get out of here and find her."

As Roger rushed off, Amory called after him irritably, "I wish the two of you would make up your minds about my offer. It could be one hell of a good book, Roger."

Driving toward Valerie's house, Roger mulled over the things Amory had told him. So Valerie had turned down the new book, after all. Why? Perhaps she wanted nothing further to do with him or his world. Perhaps she wanted to demonstrate to him that she hadn't used him to get ahead.

Of course, he never thought she had. Valerie was too genuine a person to ever use anyone. Still he'd said such thoughtless, cruel things to her at lunch. He'd been so scared then, so sure that it was best to break things off, that he'd done so hastily and had botched it up terribly. Would she ever forgive him?

Well, she had tried to find him, hadn't she? Maybe it hadn't been just to thumb her nose at him. And she had told Amory she had a different priority right now. All of this gave him new hope.

WHILE ROGER WAS ON HIS WAY out to her house, Valerie was driving around the downtown area of Natchez, consumed with turmoil. She'd been very disappointed when she went by Roger's hotel and discovered that he still hadn't returned from fishing with Rico. Having to speak with Amory Carlisle again had been awkward, too.

She had felt so much better after talking with Myrna, but now that she hadn't been able to find Roger, doubts and second thoughts had begun to seep in again. After all, her fight with him at lunch had seemed so final.

Growing tired of driving around, Valerie parked her car at the top of Silver Street and walked down into Natchez-Under-the-Hill. She went to stand at the edge of the landing, staring out at the lovely smooth river. She inhaled its comforting, earthy smell as the breeze whipped about her. She hoped the tranquil surroundings would somehow soothe her pain.

This is where it had all begun, she thought with a catch in her heart. Only six weeks ago on a beautiful starry night, she and Roger had shared their first kiss on the deck of the *Delta Princess*.

So much had happened since then. . . .

Would she be able to find him now? When she did, would he meet her halfway, or would he reject her again? Had she lost everything now—the man she loved, and her career?

AT VALERIE'S HOUSE, Roger noted that her car wasn't there. Nevertheless, he hurried up the back stairs and knocked on her door. Predictably there was no answer. He went downstairs to her dad's door, and his knock was answered by a frowning Fred Vernon.

"Mr. Vernon, do you have any idea where Valerie is?" Roger asked. "It's critical that I find her immediately."

Fred was about to reply, when a pretty, plump older woman joined him at the doorway. "Why, hello, there. You must be Valerie's friend, Mr. Benedict."

"Yes, I am," Roger replied, rather taken aback. "And you're—"

"Myrna Floyd, a friend of Valerie's—and Fred's," Myrna replied, extending her hand to Roger.

As the two shook hands, Fred said in a hostile tone, "Regarding your question, Mr. Benedict, I really have no idea where my daughter is."

"Fred!" Myrna glanced at him askance. "That's not very friendly, I must say. Aren't you even going to ask Mr. Benedict in?"

Before Fred could reply, Roger held up a hand and said, "Really, I can't stay."

"Well, I do know Valerie is looking for you," Myrna told Roger with a conspiratorial wink.

"She is?" he replied, his eyes lighting with new hope. He turned back to Fred and noted with dismay that he was still glowering. What the hell, he thought. "By the way, Mr. Vernon, I'm going to marry your daughter," he said evenly.

Now Fred Vernon stepped forward aggressively. "Mr. Benedict, I'll have you know—"

Abruptly Fred stopped in midsentence, muttering "Ouch!" as Myrna jabbed him in the ribs.

"Don't let us keep you then, Mr. Benedict," Myrna told Roger sweetly. "This is a fairly small town, after all. I'm sure you'll have no trouble finding Valerie. Invite us to the wedding, now will you?"

Roger grinned. "Of course."

Hastily making his retreat down the path, Roger chuckled to himself as he heard Myrna behind him, saying, "Now Fred Vernon, I think it's about time you and I had a talk about Valerie...." Then he heard the door to the Vernon house slam shut.

Roger went by Valerie's studio downtown and also checked back by his hotel, but still he couldn't find her. Growing distraught, he just drove around town aimlessly, desperately hoping he would spot her small car. At last, he did spot her subcompact parked at the top of Silver Street. He parked his car next to it then walked down the steep incline into Natchez-Under-the-Hill.

He found Valerie at the base of Silver Street, standing at the landing, staring out at the river as the sunset flooded it with gold. Never had she looked so beautiful to him. She wore her thick auburn hair down about her shoulders. The breeze tugged at her lush curls and the feminine blue sundress she wore. Her face was lovely, but her eyes were glazed with sadness as she stared out at the water. How he hated himself for putting that anguish there! He was tempted to grab her and kiss her senseless, but he knew there were things they had to address first.

As Roger approached, Valerie was unaware that he was about to join her. Suddenly she heard him whisper her name and felt his hands on her shoulder. "Roger," she whispered back, staring up at him with joy and uncertainty.

"Hello, darling," he told her with a tender smile. "I heard you were looking for me."

"Did you?" she asked, and there was a catch in her voice as she turned to stare back out at the river.

Roger knew a moment of near panic. Had he come too late? "You know, you've been rather hard to find yourself," he went on. "I've been all over town hunting you."

"Have you?" she whispered.

For a moment they just stood there, listening to the rustle of tree limbs above them and the laughter of a couple who were entering a restaurant behind them. Then Valerie said poignantly, "I was just looking out at the river. Remembering that night on the steamboat, remembering our first kiss. Where did we go wrong, Roger?"

Roger sighed, his hands clutching her shoulders. "We came back."

Valerie sniffed and continued, "I kept thinking that if only we could go back to the beginning and start all over again, maybe we could get it right this time. But then I thought, no, I wouldn't trade a single minute of our time together for the world."

As Valerie spoke, she began to cry. With an anguished groan, Roger turned her in his arms, clutching her tightly to him and stroking her hair. "Darling, please don't cry. I'm so sorry I hurt you today. I was such a jerk. Please try to understand that I was just scared and confused. Amory and Elaine were babbling away about their coming grandchild, and you were sitting there, so young and beautiful. I suddenly felt so removed from you, in years and in so many ways. I just felt I'd be asking you to give up too much."

"Roger, no, I—"

"Please, hear me out," he said hoarsely, staring down into her eyes. "Then when Amory started playing up to you, complimenting you on your work, my pride was chafed. I kept saying to myself, 'She's so good, so talented. Why should she need me anymore?'"

"Not need you?" Valerie repeated with a disbelieving laugh. "How could I ever not need you?"

He cupped her face with his hands. "Amory said you turned down the new assignment. He said you have a different priority right now. What is it, darling?"

Staring up at him with eyes brimming with emotion, she said, "It's you, Roger. I love you so much."

"Oh, darling, I love you, too," Roger said, kissing her. They clung to each other, pouring their emotions into the kiss. Valerie found it heavenly to be in Roger's strong arms again after the anguish of their separation.

After a moment, he continued hoarsely, "And it took the prospect of losing you to make me realize how much I love you and need you. Maybe it's selfish, but I don't care about our differences anymore. I just can't let you go."

"It's not selfish," Valerie replied, hugging him. "And I don't care about any of it, either—not the years between us or anything else. If we love each other, we'll work it out."

"Are you really sure?" he went on. "I mean, what if I can't—"

"Can't what, Roger?"

He smiled down at her. "You can be very demanding sexually."

"*I* can be demanding sexually?" she repeated indignantly. "Who wanted me three times a day out in the woods? Who took his own sweet time and just let me lie there and lie there.... Losing my mind!"

He pressed his forehead to hers as they both shook with tender laughter. "Was I that cruel, darling?" he asked.

"Yes! And I loved it." More seriously she added, "Roger, it's going to be okay. Believe me, I've worried about keeping up with *your* demands, too."

"You're kidding."

"No, I'm not." She tilted her chin slightly. "I like to sleep sometimes, just like anyone else."

He kissed her cheek, her neck. "What a darling you are! But are you really sure? Aren't there some things you'll miss?"

"Like what?"

"Like having a dozen children?"

She bit her lip, then said tentatively, "Well . . . would you mind just one?"

He smiled, then replied with a catch in his voice, "Oh, Valerie. I think that, between the two of us, we might be able to handle one."

"I'll do the 2:00 a.m. feedings—promise," she put in eagerly.

He stroked her hair away from her face and asked, "But would one child be enough for you?"

She nodded. "I'm an only child, and so are you. I never minded. Did you?"

He drew her close, tenderly kissing her temple. "I thought about having a child with you—out in the woods. I thought about it so much, wanted it so badly. Frankly, it scared the hell out of me at the time. That was an aspect of life that I'd just assumed was denied to me for so long. Now, just to think of having this second chance . . ." His voice broke, then he added with a touch of poignant humor, "But do me a favor and let's get started soon, darling. I'm not getting any younger."

"Well, don't count on me letting you off the hook any time soon, fella," Valerie replied stoutly. "I'm expecting you to be around for a long, long time." Holding him close, she whispered, "I just want to be with you, Roger. You still have so much to teach me."

Hugging her back, he said, "Oh, darling, I think you have so much more to teach me. Like how to be young again— really young at heart." Looking down into her eyes, he said, "Let's do the book set in France together. Let's get married first."

"Oh, Roger." She grinned up at him. "Do you suppose it will be romantic getting pregnant in France?"

"We'll certainly give it our best efforts," he said gravely. "Well, Ms Vernon. Is it a yes? Will you do me the honor of becoming my wife?"

She nodded. "Yes. On one condition."

He looked alarmed. "Dare I ask?"

"I'm spending the night with you at your hotel."

Roger howled with laughter. "Fine. To hell with what the rest of the world thinks. And I imagine you'll be just tickled pink if we run into Amory and Elaine in the hotel lobby, won't you?"

"Tickled pink," she said with a smirk.

"Come here, you tigress," he growled.

After a long kiss, Valerie pressed her mouth against his cheek and whispered, "I'm going to make you lose control tonight, Roger."

"Oh, my love. Don't you know you already have?" His arms trembled about her, and she felt the wetness of his tears on her face.

They held each close for a long time. Then they climbed the hill together, hand in hand.

HARLEQUIN *Temptation*

COMING NEXT MONTH

#293 THE ADENTURER Jayne Ann Krentz (Ladies and Legends, Book 2)

When romance writer Sarah Fleetwood hired ex-adventurer Gideon Trace to help her locate an old family heirloom, she got more than she bargained for. Gideon was the image of the hero she'd depicted in so many of her books—mysterious, dangerously appealing...but unavailable. Sarah had to figure out what made him tick—or forego the happy ending....

#294 ONLY HUMAN Kelly Street

Librarian Caitlin Stewart was just getting over her painful past when Lee Michaels charged through her carefully placed blocks. His investigation into football recruitment violations pointed to Caitlin's late husband. Lee would need all the right moves for the most important play of his life—getting Caitlin to love him.

#295 RIPE FOR THE PICKING Mary Tate Engels

When wounded law-enforcement officer Brett Meyer returned to his father's New Mexico ranch, he received a hero's welcome—from everyone except Annie Clayton. Annie found his presence unsettling. Her life was firmly rooted in her struggling apple farm and Brett was restless to move on. Annie feared he'd leave again...and take her heart with him.

#296 GUARDED MOMENTS JoAnn Ross

Chantal Giraudeau was a princess—and she expected everyone to treat her royally. But special agent Caine O'Bannion wasn't about to indulge her every whim. His assignment was to guard her during her American tour. And protect her, he would...even if it meant keeping watch over her day and night!

HARLEQUIN *Temptation*

The Adventurer

JAYNE ANN KRENTZ

Remember THE PIRATE (Temptation #287), the first book of Jayne Ann Krentz's exciting trilogy Ladies and Legends? Next month Jayne brings us another powerful romance, THE ADVENTURER (Temptation #293), in which Kate, Sarah and Margaret — three long-time friends featured in THE PIRATE — meet again.

A contemporary version of a great romantic myth, THE ADVENTURER tells of Sarah Fleetwood's search for long-lost treasure and for love. Only when she meets her modern-day knight-errant Gideon Trace will Sarah know she's found the path to fortune and eternal bliss....

THE ADVENTURER — available in April 1990! And in June, look for THE COWBOY (Temptation #302), the third book of this enthralling trilogy.

**In April, Harlequin brings you the
world's most popular romance author**

JANET DAILEY

No Quarter Asked

Out of print since 1974!

After the tragic death of her father, Stacy's world is shattered. She
needs to get away by herself to sort things out. She leaves behind
her boyfriend, Carter Price, who wants to marry her. However, as
soon as she arrives at her rented cabin in Texas, Cord Harris, owner
of a large ranch, seems determined to get her to leave. When Stacy
has a fall and is injured, Cord reluctantly takes her to his own ranch.
Unknown to Stacy, Carter's father has written to Cord and asked
him to keep an eye on Stacy and try to convince her to return home.
After a few weeks there, in spite of Cord's hateful treatment that
involves her working as a ranch hand and the return of Lydia, his ex-
fiancée, by the time Carter comes to escort her back, Stacy knows
that she is in love with Cord and doesn't want to go.

**Watch for *Fiesta San Antonio* in July and
For Bitter or Worse in September.**

Have You Ever Wondered If You Could Write A Harlequin Novel?

Here's great news—Harlequin is offering a series of cassette tapes to help you do just that. Written by Harlequin editors, these tapes give practical advice on how to make your characters—and your story—come alive. There's a tape for each contemporary romance series Harlequin publishes.

Mail order only

All sales final

Harlequin
Superromance®

LET THE GOOD TIMES ROLL . . .

Add some Cajun spice to liven up your New Year's celebrations and join Superromance for a romantic tour of the rich Acadian marshlands and the legendary Louisiana bayous.

CAJUN MELODIES, starting in January 1990, is a three-book tribute to the fun-loving people who've enriched America by introducing us to crawfish étouffé and gumbo, zydeco music and the Saturday night party, the *fais-dodo*. And learn about loving, Cajun-style, as you meet the tall, dark, handsome men who win their ladies' hearts with a beautiful, haunting melody. . . .

Book One: *Julianne's Song*, January 1990
Book Two: *Catherine's Song*, February 1990
Book Three: *Jessica's Song*, March 1990